36

BRO
AND
STRANGERS

Also by Marilyn Halvorson

Cowboys Don't Cry

Let It Go

Nobody Said It Would Be Easy

Dare

BROTHERS AND STRANGERS

MARILYN HALVORSON

A novel in the
Irwin Young Adult Fiction series

First published in 1991 by
Stoddart Publishing Co. Limited
34 Lesmill Road
Toronto, Canada
M3B 2T6

Canadian Cataloguing in Publication Data

Halvorson, Marilyn, 1948-
  Brothers and strangers

ISBN 0-7737-5369-9

I. Title.

PS8565.A58B7 1991   jC813'.54   C90-095900-2
PZ7.H35Br 1991

Cover Design: Brant Cowie / Artplus Ltd.
Cover Illustration: Paul McCusker
Typesetting: Jay Tee Graphics Ltd.

Printed in Canada

To
Jim and June,
my very special neighbors

One

I was a month short of sixteen when my brother came home — if you can call coming to a place you've never been coming home. A lot of water had gone under the bridge in the seven years he'd been gone. I was living with Pop instead of Mom now and he and I had moved a couple of times. For the last two years we'd been living in a rundown house on the edge of Fenton.

It was a rainy Alberta August night. It seemed like there'd been nothing but rainy nights and days that month and it was getting on my nerves. School would be starting in a couple of weeks and the summer was going to waste. Especially when the most exciting thing I had to do was wash the supper dishes, which Pop had stuck me with again. He was in the last stages of building a saddle for a guy at Pincher Creek — leather work is what he does for a living — and he wanted to get it finished so he could take it down there this weekend.

When I heard the car drive in I was up to my elbows in greasy water so I didn't go to the door. I knew who it would be anyhow. Darcy Sanderson in his burnt-out '78 Trans Am. We went cruising once in a while when there wasn't anything better to do.

I was still scraping burnt-on egg off the frypan when I heard footsteps and then a knock on the door. "Come on in," I hollered. Nothing happened.

"Geez, Sanderson," I muttered. "You deaf or somethin'? Okay, okay, I'm comin'," I yelled, wiping my hands on my jeans as I headed for the door.

I was still dripping soapsuds as I flung open the door. "Hey, Darce . . ." I stopped short. It wasn't Darcy. It was a stranger standing there with the glow of the kitchen light reflecting off his rain-wet face. For a minute, neither of us said anything. We just looked at each other.

There was something familiar about the guy. More the way he stood, the way he looked at me, than the face. But his eyes, there was something about his eyes . . .

His hair, just long enough not to have that clean-cut preppy look, was blond. That had made me expect blue eyes. But his eyes weren't blue. They were dark. Not really brown, though. More hazel. Brown and green and grey all mixed to a color like a winter creek just before it freezes. A real strange color. I could only remember seeing two people with eyes just that color. One of them was me . . .

The stranger must have been thinking in the same pattern because a slow smile started spreading across his face. He reached up and pushed his wet hair out of his eyes like he needed to be real sure of what he was seeing. "Beau?" he said softly, turning my name into a question.

I nodded slowly. "Yeah," I said, staring hard at him. "Steve?"

His smile widened. "Yeah," he said. Then he looked

me up and down one more time. "Man, you've changed since you were nine," he said.

"Well you don't exactly look like you did at twelve either," I shot back, and we both started to laugh. But that's about where the conversation died. Seven years is a big hole out of anybody's life. Last time I'd seen my brother he hadn't even been a teenager. Now he was nineteen, officially an adult. What had he done with those years in between was a question so huge I didn't know where to start asking.

I didn't get the chance anyway. It was Steve who asked the first question. "Where's the old man?"

"Out in the shop, building a saddle," I said, tossing the dish rag in the general direction of the counter. "Come on, I'll take you out there."

Steve shook his head. "No," he said. "I think I'd better talk to him alone."

That stopped me dead in my tracks. I stood there, waiting for the explanation that never came. Steve just said, "See you later, Beau," and walked back out into the rain, leaving me standing there, staring at the closed door and wondering crazily if my brother had really been here at all.

He was out there for a long time. Long enough for me to finish the dishes, straighten up the kitchen, sweep the floor, and do enough thinking to get about half mad at him. What was the big deal anyhow with all this top-secret, got-to-see-Pop-alone stuff, I thought, as I wiped the table off. What did he think — that he'd done all the growing up these past seven years and I was still nine years old? Well, he could forget that idea. I'd grown up some, too.

Pop didn't treat me like a kid. Heck, a lot of the time he didn't treat me like much of anything in particular. I was just there and so was he. It wasn't exactly the

Cosby family but it wasn't so bad. In fact, it was a whole lot better than it used to be, back in those last few months when we were a whole family — when Steve was still there, and Mom. Back when Pop had just lost the ranch and we had to move to Calgary. Mom was always yelling at Pop 'cause there was never enough money. Pop mostly wouldn't answer at all and just sat there staring at the TV all evening like he was stone deaf. And then Steve started getting in trouble in school all the time and the principal would phone and say that somebody better get down to the school and talk to him or he was going to kick Steve out for good. And then Mom and Pop would fight over who was going to go and they'd both end up yelling at Steve and he'd take off and stay out all night and then they'd yell at each other over whose fault it was if he got murdered or run over by a freight train . . .

And then there was me, good old bright-eyed Beau, thinking all the time that if I just got better marks and did all my chores around the house and never did anything to make waves I was going to single-handedly keep the Garrett family boat from sinking.

I might as well have saved my energy, I thought bitterly, noticing that I'd just scrubbed a rose right off the dingy plastic tablecloth. The summer before I turned nine it all fell apart. Mom got a divorce — and custody of me. She let Pop take Steve — or the way I see it now, made Pop take him. She'd given up on him by then . . .

I was so deep in the past that I must have jumped a foot in the air when the door suddenly burst open. I spun around and there was Steve, a rolled-up sleeping bag thrown over his shoulder, a gym bag in his hand, and a great big grin plastered across his face. "Hey, Beau!" he said.

"Hey, what?" I snapped, not being in the world's best mood.

Steve didn't seem to notice that detail. He just strolled in, leaving a trail of muddy bootprints across the floor I'd just swept, and threw his stuff on the first chair he came to. "You just got yourself a live-in brother," he announced, like I'd won first prize in a million-dollar lottery.

I didn't answer. I just walked over to the back closet and picked up the floor rag. "Think fast," I said as I winged it at him as hard as I could. He caught it. Whatever he'd been doing for the past seven years he still had the same old cat reflexes.

"What's this?" he said blankly, staring at the rag in his hand with an expression so amazed you'd think I'd handed him a laser gun and asked him to perform brain surgery with it.

I nodded to the tracks on the floor. "We don't have a maid," I said.

For a second I thought he might throw the rag right back in my face but then he just laughed. "Sure, Beau," he said with a shrug. "Guess I'm gonna have to get domesticated around here." He bent over and started scrubbing — sort of. One thing for sure, whatever he'd been doing all the time he'd been gone, it hadn't included cleaning house.

He finished, hung the muddy rag over the oven door handle — right on top of the dish towel — and then looked up with a grin. "Okay. Now what?"

I couldn't help it. I grinned back. Staying mad at him was just too much trouble. "Now," I said, "we go and bring in your stuff."

"I just did," he said.

I looked at the gym bag on the chair. "That's all the clothes you got?"

Steve gave me a kind of funny look and for a second I thought he was going to start explaining something. But then he just shrugged. "Sure," he said, "that's enough. Unless I'm gonna need my tux to keep up with the social life around here."

I laughed. "Not much danger. Come on. We'll throw this stuff in my bedroom."

Two

The house wasn't very big. Neither was my bedroom. There was room for the bed — which was a double one, mainly because it had already been there when we moved in — a table, and the dresser. But there was one thing about the room I really liked. A bench, built right in by the window. Being upstairs, you could sit there and look all over the country. Lately I'd looked at a lot of rain.

Steve glanced around the little room. "Hey, Beau," he said, "I don't mean to crowd you out. I can throw my sleeping bag on the couch downstairs."

"You're not crowding me any," I said, wondering if I was telling the truth. I'd had my own space for a long time now. Sharing it again was going to seem pretty weird. But, thinking it over, I realized that Steve being gone all that time had left a big hole in my life. I really did want to get to know my brother again.

"Okay, if you're sure it's all right," Steve said. He wandered over to the window, looked out into the rainy evening and then did a tour of the room — which involved walking about three steps in each direction. Then he spotted my guitar standing in the corner behind the dresser. He picked it up. "You play this?" he asked, strumming a couple of experimental chords.

"Yeah," I said, kind of embarrassed, "a little."

"Country, I suppose?" and something in his voice turned the question into a challenge.

"Is there anything else?"

He just laughed and shook his head. "Not for you, I guess."

"So," I said, "I guess that means you don't play country, huh?"

He shook his head slowly — and then all of a sudden he belted out a couple of licks that must have sent my poor old guitar into a state of shock. "Rock till you drop!" he yelled.

He turned to put the guitar back and I just sat there on the bed, thinking. Thinking about how opposite we were in so many ways — and about how much the same we were too. Seven years ago neither one of us had ever laid our hands on a guitar. Now we were both playing them . . .

Steve paced the room, restless as ever. "So, uh, Beau, what do you do around here for excitement?"

I shrugged. "Not a whole lot. Between rodeos anyhow."

He stopped pacing and turned to look at me. "You started rodeoing?"

"Yeah, some. Mostly just high school stuff. Entered the novice bareback at a few rodeos this summer."

Steve shook his head. "You ain't got any more sense than the old man."

"What's that supposed to mean?"

"You're the one that lives with him, Beau. I shouldn't have to draw you pictures. Ten years of riding broncs and what did it get him? A drawer full of silver buckles and a bad leg. That's all he's got left to show for it. Rodeoing lost him everything he cared about. His ranch and . . .'' His voice trailed off and he stood with his back to me, staring out the window.

''And his wife.'' I finished the sentence for him.

Steve turned around and I tried to read his face as he shook his head. ''Yeah,'' he said, his voice soft, ''but he'd have lost her anyway.''

I didn't say anything. What was there to say? Steve was right. Mom hadn't been the staying kind. Not with a guy like Pop.

Steve broke the silence. ''So how's Mom doing anyhow? She still married to her real estate man?''

''Yeah. At least she was at Easter. That's the last I heard from her. They got two kids now.''

''Yeah? She like 'em any better than she liked the first two?''

I studied my brother's face, looking for the bitterness that must be behind those words. But I didn't find it. I guessed the time for that was long gone. Now Steve was just telling it the way it was — or at least the way he saw it. That, to Mom, the thirteen years she spent married to Pop and raising us had been a total waste. Maybe it was true. I never understood how she and Pop got together in the first place. They weren't just from different worlds, they were from different planets. Mom wanted things — nice, expensive things so people would think she had class. Pop never cared what anyone thought. All he wanted was to be free. Well, maybe they'd both finally come close . . .

Suddenly I didn't want to talk about the past anymore. I didn't even want to think about it. ''Hey,'' I said, ''I forgot to tell you. I've got a job.''

''Yeah? Doin' what? Pumpin' gas?'' Steve's tone was

kind of bored, like I was too much of a kid to do anything better.

"No," I said, defensively, "training horses."

I expected that would probably be too tame for this cool stranger who used to be my brother, but I was wrong. One thing hadn't changed since the time we had the ranch. Horses still mattered to Steve. "No kiddin'," he said, with a certain amount of respect. "Where?"

"Kincade's Quarter Circle. It's just down the road." And then, because I figured he was going to find out anyway, I added, "Well, I don't really get to do that much training. They've got a professional trainer. Mainly, I do a lot of shovelling."

Steve laughed. "What kind of horses they got?"

"Quarter."

"Good ones?"

"Yeah, some of them. Especially Rebel Yell, the new stallion they just brought in from Texas. He's got a pedigree a mile long from racing-quarter-horse stock and he's supposed to be about the fastest thing on four legs."

"What do you mean 'supposed to be'? Has he won any races?"

"Not yet. Nobody's been able to stay on him long enough to get him running in a straight line. He's bucked Russ Donovan off every time he's got on so far." Which, I could have added, always made my day. Russ Donovan, Kincade's big-time trainer, wasn't one of my favorite people.

"So," Steve said thoughtfully, "I guess disposition wasn't included in the Rebel's mile-long pedigree."

"He's still a good horse," I said. Steve didn't need to land here out of nowhere and start running Kincade's horses down.

"Hey, I never said he wasn't," he said with a tolerant grin. "Bein' mean as sin don't have nothin' to do

with whether you're good or not." He was u₁
around again, restless as a caged cat. Suddenly
thing on the dresser caught his eye. He picked it ₁   ₁u
gave a low whistle. "Who is *this*, little brother?" he
asked, holding up the picture I'd had leaning against
the mirror.

"That's, uh, my girlfriend," I said, feeling my face
do a slow burn.

"What's her name?"

"Raine Kincade."

Steve gave me a look. "Kincade as in Kincade's
Quarter Circle?" he asked.

I nodded. "You got it," I said. "She's J.C. Kincade's
daughter."

Steve shook his head. "The boss's daughter," he said
admiringly. "How long you been goin' out with her?"

I sort of shrugged. "I dunno. A few months," I said,
being careful not to let him pin me down. The fact was
we didn't really "go out" together that much at all —
except to rodeos a lot. Mostly we just worked together
and rode together. Stuff like that. I guess Raine and me
were actually more like best friends. But I hadn't exactly
lied to Steve about us. She was a friend and nobody
could ever deny that she was a girl. That kind of made
her a girlfriend, didn't it?

I figured I'd answered enough questions. It was
Steve's turn to answer a few. "So," I said, "where have
you been all this time?"

For a minute he didn't answer and I wondered if he
was going to answer at all. Then, "Oh, around. Vancouver mostly," he said.

He set the picture down, walked over to the window,
and stared out. Then he turned back to me. "Come on,
Beau, let's get out of here."

"Out of here where?"

"I don't know. Just out. I'll take you for a ride in my car."

Good old Steve. He'd been gone seven years and back half an hour and already he was bored. But I wasn't about to argue. *I'd* been here long enough to appreciate a change of scenery.

"Sure," I said, heading for the stairs.

I grabbed my jean jacket off the hook beside the door and we went outside. The rain had stopped and it smelled good out now. I took a glance in the direction of Pop's shop, wondering if I should stick my head in the door and tell him we were going. No, I was too old for that stuff. Yesterday I probably wouldn't have been, but now I was with Steve. Somehow that made me a whole lot older.

Besides, right then I got my first good look at Steve's car. For a minute I just stared. It looked like it belonged in the movies — and it sure didn't belong in a place like Fenton. It was an old Dodge, mid-sixties I guessed, but the year was the only thing that was old. Somebody had spent a pile of time and money restoring it, so now it sat gleaming in the early dusk like a polished thoroughbred. Except for the color, that is. A horse that color had never been born. As a matter of fact, not many *cars* that color had ever been born.

I turned to look at Steve. He was standing there with a half-smile twitching the corners of his mouth, watching my reaction. "Hey," I said, "I like your mauve car!"

He gave me a dirty look. "Mauve? That ain't *mauve*. That's Plum Crazy Purple. I repainted her the original color and if you don't believe me I've got the color chart to prove it."

I shrugged. "Still looks mauve to me. Do I get to drive?"

"Not likely, kid," Steve said, sliding behind the wheel. "Get in or you get to walk."

I got in. Steve turned the key and the car's engine woke up with a menacing growl. This could turn out to be an interesting ride.

Steve stopped at the end of the driveway. "So, which way is it to town?"

"Left," I said.

He turned right. "Left, I said. Haven't you learned to tell them apart yet?" Steve never could remember left from right when he was a kid. Maybe it was because he was left-handed.

Now he just gave me an infuriating grin, took both hands off the wheel and studied them intently while the Dodge started heading for the ditch. "Gee, Beau, guess not," he said seriously. "Is the left one on the east side?"

I smothered a squawk as the right front tire hit the grass at the edge of the ditch. Casually, Steve dropped a hand to the wheel and herded the car back onto the road. Then he looked at me and laughed. "Lighten up, Beau, you're too young to get an ulcer."

"Yeah, and I'm also too young to be a traffic fatality," I muttered. But, I had to admit it, I was having fun. I'd almost forgot what it was like to have a big brother. I sat there watching him drive, fast but cool and in control as the Dodge devoured the highway. There were a few thousand questions I wanted to ask him but I didn't know where to start. I never did get started because right then we sizzled past Kincade's gate.

"That's where I work," I said, thinking Steve would be interested. I was right — but I hadn't counted on *how* interested. Instantly, he hit the brake and almost threw us into a total tailspin. "What are you doin'?" I asked, after I'd removed my teeth from the dashboard.

"Stoppin'," Steve said calmly. "I want to see this place."

I stared at him. "*Now?*"

"No, yesterday. Why, what's the matter with now?"

I looked at my watch. "It's a quarter after nine."

Steve sighed, leaned back in the seat, and gave me kind of a pitying look. "Beau," he said tiredly, "I realize we're talking Fenton and all, but do people *really* go to bed at 8:30 here?"

I felt my face do a slow burn. "No, but . . ."

"Good," he said, turning into the driveway. "Then let's go see Kincade's Quarter Circle." He paused long enough to flash me a sideways look and a wicked grin. "I gotta have a look at those quarter horses."

I was still digesting that remark when, way down the long, muddy lane, I noticed the car coming toward us. Great timing. There was room for two cars to pass — just — and that was in good weather. I hoped Steve knew what he was doing. With those wide, smooth tires of his, if he pulled over too far we were going to land in the ditch. And I did not want to have to get J.C. Kincade to pull us out . . .

Right about then I recognized the other vehicle. It wasn't a car at all. It was a black and silver four-by-four half-ton and it was coming at us through the misty dusk like a bat straight out of hell, spraying up sheets of muddy water as it fishtailed back and forth across the lane.

With a sudden jolt of panic I realized that the driver wasn't planning to share the road. It was hit the ditch or Steve's pretty purple car was going to get made into plum jam. I shot Steve a nervous glance but his eyes were on the four-by-four. He held the car steady on the road and flashed his lights a couple of times. "Steve,"

I said, fighting to keep my voice level, "he's not gonna move over."

"Yes he is," Steve said. His voice was calm. So was his face. He was almost smiling. I watched in disbelief as he held the car steady in the tracks and sped up a little.

A lot of stuff went through my mind in the next second or two but it wasn't my life flashing before me like they say happens when you're about to die. Mostly, I thought about how mad I was at the guy in the truck. It was Russ Donovan, J.C.'s horse trainer. I'd always known he was a jerk but I didn't know he was a homicidal jerk.

But I was just as mad at my brother. He'd been home for an hour and I was already in more trouble than I'd been in all the time he was gone. He was about to get us both killed for no better reason than he was too proud to back down. He hadn't changed one bit.

The truck was so close I could see the space between Donovan's front teeth. I closed my eyes and braced for the impact.

It never came. There was a squeal of brakes. The Dodge's engine roared and the car swerved wildly. Then we weren't moving anymore . . .

I opened my eyes cautiously. To my amazement we weren't upside down in the ditch or mashed like bugs into the grill of the four-by-four. We were sitting neatly in the middle of the road. Steve looked over at me and grinned. "Feelin' okay, Beau?" he asked.

I gave him a dirty glare. "Where's Donovan?"

"If that's the name of the genius in the truck, check the ditch."

I swung around and looked behind us, just in time to see Donovan pile out of the truck, aim a vicious kick at its crumpled fender, and start heading in our direction.

Steve saw him coming. And the look on my brother's face as he reached for the door handle took me back seven years in one second. I'd seen that look so many times and I knew what it meant. If Donovan wanted to fight, he'd come to the right guy.

Three

Nothing would have given me more pleasure than to watch Donovan and Steve pound each other's empty heads into the mud — or so I thought until I saw something that changed my mind completely. Standing down by the barn, his bulk unmistakable even in the fading light, was none other than J.C. Kincade himself.

Oh no, I thought, feeling my stomach lurch, J.C. had been taking in this interesting little demolition derby, which was nothing compared to the main event he was about to witness, with Donovan and Steve going at it right in the middle of the road. J.C. wasn't exactly a laid-back kind of guy. He didn't like it when things got out of hand and he wasn't going to like this one little bit.

Considering J.C.'s disposition, Beau Garrett getting a job at Kincade's Quarter Circle had been nothing short of a miracle. Pop and me didn't exactly come with a high-society pedigree, and J.C. had given me a lecture a mile long about how he didn't want any punks or ruffians (I loved that word) anywhere near his ranch —

or his daughter. It was Raine's mom that finally loosened old J.C. up enough to try me out for the job last spring. I'd been walking on eggs ever since, trying not to irritate him. And now I was about to land right in the middle of one *big* irritation. I had to do something fast or say goodbye to my job, my five bucks an hour, and worst of all, to the first, best-looking, and only almost-girlfriend I'd ever had.

"Don't do it, Steve!" I blurted out, grabbing his arm.

He jerked loose. "Stay out of this, Beau!"

I knew better than to get in his way when he was in a mood like this but right now I had more important things to save than the present arrangement of my face. "Look, Steve," I said desperately, "that's J.C. himself over there eyeballing us and trying to figure out what's going on in his driveway."

"So?" Steve threw a smouldering look over his shoulder as he opened the door.

"So he's my boss. I need this job and I busted myself getting it and it's the best thing that ever happened to me so why don't you do me just one favor in your whole miserable life and not screw it all up by picking a fight with J.C.'s horse trainer right in his own front yard." I stopped, out of breath, and glared right back at my big brother.

His look turned incredulous. "*Pick* a fight?" he echoed. "You don't want me to *pick* a fight? Hey, Beau, you been smokin' bad dope or what? The guy tries to run *me* off the road and now *I'm* the one pickin' a fight. Get real, Beau!"

I looked over my shoulder. Donovan was almost to the car. "Steve, please . . ." He hesitated, his hand still on the door handle. He glanced in the mirror at Donovan, then back at me. Our eyes met and held for a long second.

Donovan reached out to jerk the door wide open —
but he never got the chance. Steve slammed it in his face.
Through the half-open window I could hear Donovan
swearing a blue streak and threatening Steve with everything under the sun. Steve looked at him. "Later," was
all that he said, but somehow it seemed more dangerous than all Donovan's threats.

Suddenly he slammed the Dodge into gear and hit the
gas. The wide tires spun wildly, clawing for a grip and
spraying liquid mud over everything around them —
including Russ Donovan. Big, mean Russ Donovan,
standing in the middle of the road, dripping mud and
yelling something that was lost in the roar of the engine.
It was so beautiful I had to smile.

But that smile faded fast as Steve, still explosive as
a shaken can of Coke, screeched the car to a stop right
in front of J.C. and opened the door. J.C., red-faced
and practically steaming through his Stetson, stared at
Steve and his purple car as if they'd just arrived from
outer space — and landed in a No Parking zone. "What
was that all about, down the lane there?" he demanded,
glancing in that direction just in time to see Donovan
roar the truck out of the ditch and go rocketing down
the driveway so fast he almost missed the corner onto
the highway. "Who are you anyway and what are you
doing here at this time of night?"

See, Steve, I thought, they *do* close down at 8:30.

Steve got out of the car. "That idiot that works for
you could use some driver education," he said coolly,
his voice not showing the kind of respect J.C. was used
to. He pulled a pack of cigarettes out of his pocket and
lighted one. I looked at him, standing there, arrogant
as all-get-out in his black leather jacket, leaning on his
blast-from-the-past car, and looking like he'd come
straight out of an old James Dean movie.

I got out of the car. J.C. saw me. I started to say something. He started to say something. We both stopped. Then, before either one of us could start up again, Raine came tearing around the corner of the barn, her long strawberry-blond hair flying in the wind. "Dad!" she hollered, trying to catch her breath, "he's gone over another fence."

I didn't have a clue what she was talking about, but whatever it was, she was some upset. Without even stopping to say hi, she had turned and started running back toward the darkening pasture.

J.C. seemed to understand. He swore under his breath and muttered something I couldn't hear — except that it ended with "Donovan." I was beginning to get a strong feeling that Steve and I had come into the theatre halfway through the movie. Whatever was going on, I had a suspicion that Donovan roaring out of here like a bear with his tail on fire had something to do with it. And I was planning to find out what right now. "Wait for me, Raine!" I yelled. As I started to run, I caught a glimpse of J.C. lumbering after me. Steve hadn't moved. He was still just leaning against the car, taking in all the action with this kind of amused expression like he was watching The Three Stooges or something.

I caught up to Raine just outside the pasture fence. "Raine!" I yelled between breaths. "What's goin' on?"

She threw a glance over her shoulder. "It's Rebel, Beau," she said, and kept running. She climbed halfway up the fence and stood leaning over the top rail, staring across the shadowy pasture. I climbed up beside her.

At first I couldn't see what she was looking at. But I could hear the hoofbeats. Galloping in short spurts.

Stopping. Trotting. Then breaking into a gallop again.
I focused in on the sound — and then I saw him. Just
a movement at first, then a shape. A moving black blur
just one shade darker than the deepening shadows at
the far end of the small field. Rebel Yell. Racing back
and forth along the far fence, pausing to shatter the night
with a wild, spine-chilling whinny, and then running
again. Up and down the fenceline, searching for a way
to get through — or over — that fence to the horses
grazing on the other side.

"Raine, what's . . ." I began, but I never got it finished. She swung around to face me, her eyes flashing
hot enough to scorch something. "I told him you can't
beat a horse like Rebel into anything." Her voice
sounded like she might start bawling but was trying
awful hard not to.

I put my arm around her shoulder and felt the tension running through her. "Start at the beginning,
Raine," I said softly.

She nodded, took a deep breath, and got her voice
under control. "Donovan." She said his name like it
was a dirty word. "You know what he's like when he
gets mad." I nodded. I'd had the bad luck to be the *reason* he got mad a few times. "He had Rebel in the little
corral behind the arena, trying to ride him," she said.
"Rebel dumped him in three jumps the first time." A
sudden smile flickered across her face. "You should have
seen that horse buck, Beau." The smile faded. "But
Donovan got back on. Rebel started bucking again. The
$50,000 Finals horses at the Calgary Stampede could
have taken lessons from him. But this time Donovan
stayed with him. I hate to admit it," she said grudgingly, "but the guy can ride. Rebel was getting winded
and I really thought he was going to give up this time.
Then, all of a sudden, just like he'd thought it all

through, Rebel jumped sideways and slammed Donovan's leg against the fence with all his weight. That shook Donovan loose.

"He hit the ground cussing and came up breathing fire. I'd never seen him so mad. He grabbed a whip and went after Rebel with it. I tried to stop him but it was like I wasn't even there." Raine's voice was getting rough-edged again.

"It was awful, Beau. He had Rebel cornered against the fence and he just kept hitting him. I thought he was going to kill him." She stopped, swallowed hard, and went on. "But all of a sudden, right from a standing start, Rebel went over that five-plank corral fence. I still wouldn't believe he could do it if I hadn't seen it. He didn't go clear, though. He caught the top plank and smashed it to pieces, snagged a stirrup, and almost tore the saddle off. He's running around out there with what's left of it hanging underneath him now. Then he took off across the big corral and took that fence, too."

"Yeah," I said, staring at the dim shape running up and down the pasture fence, "and in about a minute he's gonna take that one, too."

"He'd better not," Raine said, her voice almost a whisper. "That one's wire. It's so dark he'll never be able to judge the height. And if he hits it . . ."

Her voice trailed into silence. We'd both seen horses that had tried to jump barbed-wire fences. It wasn't something you wanted to see again.

Suddenly Raine started to climb over the fence. "We've got to get him out of there," she said.

"No," J.C.'s hoarse voice rasped through the near-darkness. He had come up behind us and was standing staring across the pasture, so out of breath he could hardly talk. "Leave him alone. He's so spooked now that if anyone goes near him he'll take the fence for sure. Just stay away from him.''

''But . . .'' Raine began, but then she sighed and shook her head. It was no use arguing with J.C. Maybe he was right. But then again, maybe while we all just stood here gawking Rebel was going to jump . . .

For a minute none of us said anything. We just listened to Rebel's hoofbeats and watched the darkness deepen. The sky was clearing. A few stars shone through the holes in the ragged clouds, their faint glow above making it seem even darker down here.

''What was that?'' Raine whispered.

''What?''

''Listen.''

This time I heard it too. A voice, low and distant. Coming from the same direction as the hoofbeats. The hoofbeats paused for a second and I heard Rebel snort, a sound so wild it sent shivers up my back. Then he was trotting again.

This time the voice was clearer, still low and gentle, but strong enough to carry across the rhythm of the hoofbeats. ''Whoa, Rebel. Easy boy. It's okay, Reb. Whoa now.'' The voice kept talking. The same words over and over. Soft but firm. A voice that sounded real familiar.

The hoofbeats slowed, then stopped. Rebel snorted again, still spooked and suspicious, but not so wild as before.

All three of us just stood there, listening, hypnotized by the sound of the voice down there in the darkness. I could see the scene being played out between human and horse so clearly in my mind that it took me a few seconds to realize that, suddenly, I really *could* see it. Moonlight was spilling through a hole in the clouds and turning the world to a silvery blue, like the picture on an old black and white TV set. And across the pasture I saw exactly what I knew I was going to see. A blond kid in a black leather jacket reaching out to a trembling jet black horse.

His hand touched Rebel's neck. Rebel snorted and took a step backward. I heard Steve's voice again, so soft now that I couldn't make out the words. He stepped forward, still holding out his hand. This time Rebel cautiously reached out to sniff it. Slowly, Steve laid his hand on the side of the horse's face and then began inching it sideways until his fingers were scratching the sweaty, itchy spot under the cheek strap of the bridle. I could almost see the tension radiating out of Rebel's body like heat waves rising on a hot summer day.

Gradually, Steve's hand moved down the bridle until he was holding what was left of the broken reins. "Come on, Rebel," he said calmly, turning and starting to walk away like there was no doubt in his mind that the horse would follow. Rebel hesitated, tossing his head up and down a couple of times, testing the hand on the reins. Then he took a step forward. Then another. And another. Following Steve so close his nose was almost touching his shoulder.

I breathed a huge sigh of relief — and wondered how long I'd been holding my breath. "Beau, who *is* that guy?" I almost jumped at the sound of Raine's voice. For a minute I'd forgotten she was there. "That's my brother," I said, and those words had never felt better than they did right then.

Four

The next thing I knew, Raine was going over the fence and I was right behind her. Behind us, J.C. was muttering something about staying back in case we spooked that outlaw horse into busting loose again.

Steve never looked in our direction as we came walking up, slow and easy, and I wasn't sure he even knew we were there until he held the reins out toward me. "Here," he said in the same quiet voice he used with Rebel. "Hold him while I get the saddle off."

He eased his way around to the side and started trying to uncinch what was left of the battered saddle. Rebel showed the whites of his eyes and started dancing sideways. "Whoa, Rebel," I said softly, trying to capture some of Steve's magic in my voice.

"Easy, Reb," Raine said, instinctively stepping around to the opposite side of the horse to keep him from edging away from Steve. I wished I could have read the look Steve shot in her direction, but it was too dark.

He bent over to work on the cinch again. Finally he gave up.

"Cinch knot's so tight it might as well be welded," he said. "Have to cut it." He reached in his pocket — for a jackknife, I figured. I figured wrong. All of a sudden there was a click and a six-inch steel blade miraculously appeared in his hand. I heard Raine take a sudden deep breath and I caught myself standing there with my mouth open. Steve didn't look up. He just slipped his hand between the horse and the strap and started sawing the knife's razor edge through the leather.

I could feel Raine's eyes on me, asking questions, but since I didn't have any answers I just concentrated on keeping the horse happy.

Steve put the knife away and pulled off the ruined saddle just as J.C. ignored his own advice and came trudging up. "Here's your saddle," Steve said, depositing the wreck in his arms.

J.C. dumped it on the ground. "Forget the saddle," he growled. "It's the horse I'm concerned about. Bring him up where I can look him over." I couldn't help but smile. That was J.C. for you. Always the big-time horseman, giving orders and expecting them to be followed. But when it came right down to handling horses, he usually managed to stay out of the way. That's what he had Donovan for.

A hot rush of anger swept through me at the thought of Donovan. This wasn't the first horse he'd abused. I knew it and Raine knew it. She'd tried to tell J.C., but horse trainers were hard to come by . . .

This time, though, Donovan had gone too far. I didn't think even J.C. would be able to look the other way now.

That train of thought was derailed by Raine. "Hold him still a second, Beau. He's favoring his right front leg. I think it's cut." She bent down and started to run her hand down the leg.

The next thing I knew I was practically dangling from the reins as Rebel gave a squeal of pain and fury and reared to his full height. I hung on for all I was worth and tried not to think about the hard black hoofs pawing the air above my head. That kept me so busy that I almost missed the real action.

"Look out!" I heard Steve yell at Raine as he grabbed her arm and dragged her back out of range of Rebel's hoofs. "You're going to get your head kicked in if you're not careful."

I had barely managed to bring Rebel back to earth when there was a resounding smack that almost spooked him all over again. At first I couldn't believe what had just happened, but on second thought, knowing Raine like I did, I could believe it. She had just hauled off and slapped Steve right across the face.

"Let go of me!" The words practically sizzled as she jerked free of his grasp. "I've seen enough two-bit macho cowboys tonight to last me a lifetime. I can take care of myself without you playing hero."

I shot a look at Steve. With his temper, I didn't know what to expect. I didn't figure anybody, male or female, hit him and got away with it.

For a minute he just stood there with this kind of amazed look on his face and thoughtfully rubbed his hand across his cheek. Then he grinned. "Not bad," he said arrogantly. "For a girl, that is. Good thing you aren't a boy. You might be dangerous."

I was sure, right then, that if Raine could have reached him she would have hit him again. Instead, she let him have it with another avalanche of words. "And who do you think you are, anyway, just dropping in here out of nowhere and taking over like you own the place? Well, I've got news for you, whatever your name is, this is my place, not yours, and when I need you to look after me I'll rattle your chain."

"Sorry," Steve said. He was still smiling but there was an edge to his voice now. "I forgot. You're the boss's daughter. So if you want to get your head kicked in, you can."

"Hurry up and get that horse up here." J.C.'s shout from the barn cut off Raine's reply. Fortunately, I think.

"Move it, Beau," Steve said. "You've been around here long enough to know that when the Kincades speak the peasants are supposed to jump. I'll go open the gate." He walked on ahead.

Slowly — because the horse was limping pretty bad — and silently — because Raine didn't seem to have anything left to say and I thought it was safer to keep my mouth shut — Raine and I walked Rebel toward the barn. Suddenly, I noticed a dark smear on Raine's hand. I reached for it. Raine looked kind of startled, but at least she didn't haul off and belt *me* one. "Did Rebel catch you with his hoof?" I asked, searching her hand for a cut.

She shook her head impatiently. "No, that's Rebel's blood. He's got a terrible cut above his knee. I touched it. That's why he went crazy like that. Which," she added disgustedly, "I was about to explain when the Hell's Angel up there grabbed me."

I looked at Steve up ahead opening the gate, the metal studs on his jacket gleaming dully in the moonlight, and wondered if Raine was thinking about that jacket — or his personality. "His name's Steve," I said.

"I could think of better ones," Raine said through her teeth.

We put Rebel in a box stall in the barn and I got my

first good look at his leg. It was wet with blood that was still oozing from a ragged hole above his knee. J.C. took one look at it, turned pale, and went to call the vet. In a minute he was back, looking even paler. "Vet's been called out of town on a family emergency," he said grimly. "I'll have to try and get one out from Calgary in the morning. There's nothing we can do till then."

Steve pushed himself away from the wall he'd been leaning on. "Sure there is," he said, his eyes on the horse.

J.C. eyed him warily. "What have you got in mind?"

"Well, at least we can find out if anything's broken. Clean out the cut and keep the swelling down. That don't take a vet."

J.C. shook his head. "Not a chance. You'll never get near that leg without tranquilizing him first."

Steve shrugged. "Never hurts to try."

Remembering Rebel's reaction when Raine touched his leg, I wasn't so sure about that. Neither was J.C. "I don't know," he grumbled, taking off his hat to wipe his sweating face. "I paid twenty thousand for that horse. I'm not sure I want anyone but a professional working on him."

"Yeah?" Steve's voice was so cool it burned. "Then maybe you should get your professional trainer back here and let him finish the job he started."

J.C.'s face turned a shade redder and I wasn't sure if it was from anger or embarrassment. But he backed down. "Okay," he said grudgingly. "See what you can do. But don't hold me responsible if he breaks your neck."

Steve gave J.C. a level look. "I don't hold you responsible for anything," he said. Then before J.C. could think that through, he added, "Get me some warm water, antiseptic, leg bandages, and ice."

For a minute J.C. just stood there with his mouth open. But then, to my total amazement, he turned and hurried off in the direction of the house.

Steve turned to Raine, who'd been keeping dangerously quiet and eyeing him like he was a rattlesnake in the oat bin. "Well, boss's daughter," he said tauntingly, "since this is *your* place, do you think you can find a halter to fit this horse?"

"Yeah," she said sweetly. "I can do that." Then her eyes narrowed and the next words came out like she was spitting icicles. "But if you ever call me *that* again, you'll be *wearing* that halter, Rebel without a Cause!" She tossed her head and flounced off toward the tackroom.

Steve looked at me. "Thought you said the horse's name was Rebel *Yell*," he said innocently.

"It is, Steve. She wasn't talkin' to the horse."

We had the bridle off and the halter on by the time J.C. got back with the stuff. Steve took off his jacket and bent over for a closer look at the leg. He reached out his hand — he hadn't even touched the leg yet — when, like lightning, Rebel's ears went back and he swung his head around to take a vicious bite at him. Steve jumped back as the stallion's teeth came together with an ominous clunk.

Steve laughed. "Missed me, Rebel. You'll have to be faster than that." I didn't see what he had to laugh about. Rebel had taken half the shoulder out of Steve's Billy Idol T-shirt. If that was missing, I'd hate to see what happened when he didn't miss.

I shortened up my hold on the halter as Steve stepped in to try again. "Watch yourself, Beau," he said. "This might get a little active." Then he grinned and added, "Just keep rememberin' how much you like playing cowboys."

I didn't have time to decide if that was an insult or not because, right then, things *did* get active. In the next few minutes there was more action in that stall than in a tag-team match on Wrestlemania. Just trying to keep the horse where he was supposed to be, and keeping me where he couldn't reach me, was a full-time job. Rebel raised so much dust I couldn't see, let alone breathe.

When Steve finally straightened up he looked like he'd been plowing in a dust storm and breathing like he'd run the marathon, but he was smiling. "Nothin' broke," he said. "I've got the wound cleaned out and packed with ice. That'll keep the swelling down and keep it from getting infected. I don't think there's any permanent damage. He should be ready to work in a week or two."

J.C. shook his head. "I don't plan to have him around in a week or two. Fellow offered me fifteen thousand for him last week. I'm going to call him up and see if he's still interested, cut my losses, and unload this outlaw before he kills himself or somebody else."

I was watching Raine — as usual — when he said that. Her face went white. "No, Dad . . ." she began in sort of a choked voice.

"There's nothing wrong with the horse," Steve cut in, "except that he's been mishandled so bad he's gone sour on the whole world."

"So this is where everybody is." A woman's voice broke in, shattering the tension. "What on earth is going on out here? And where did that purple car come from?" Raine's mom, I thought, with a sigh of relief. When she was around, things usually lightened up real fast.

Instantly, Steve's mood changed. "Told you it was purple," he said, giving me a wink. "It's mine," he said, turning to Mary Kincade "You like it?" he asked, grinning like a little kid with a new wagon.

For a minute, Mary didn't say anything. I could see her sizing up my brother. Then she nodded. "Sure," she said. "It's got character. I like that." That was the truth. Mary and J.C. were about as different as two people could get. He liked things — and people — to be neat and orderly, rotating in their places like well-oiled ball-bearings, but Mary liked things that were unique and interesting. She got a kick out of crazy situations — which was just as well, since she was a junior high school teacher.

More than once I'd heard Pop say that anyone who thinks he's a big-time horse breeder had better be married to someone with a real job. I always thought that was kind of funny 'cause he could have just as well filled in "rodeo cowboy" instead of "horse breeder."

Anyway, as far as I could figure out about the Kincades, Pop had probably been right. They seemed to have a pretty well-balanced budget. Mary made money and J.C. spent it.

I was still thinking about that when Mary spotted the bandage on Rebel's leg. "Rebel!" she said. "What on earth have you done to yourself now?"

Rebel wasn't saying much right then but that was no problem. Raine made up for it, giving her the whole story about Rebel and Donovan, hardly stopping for breath. It was all what she'd already told me — except for one last thing. "And," she ended, breathlessly, "Dad fired Donovan right on the spot. Was he ever mad!"

That news didn't faze Mary one little bit. She just nodded. "Good," she said. "It was well past time to get rid of him." Then, all of a sudden, she shifted the focus onto me. "Well, Beau," she said cheerfully, "aren't you going to introduce me to your friend?"

That kind of took me by surprise. I'm not real good at all those mannerly things anyway, and somehow I got the strong impression that there were at least two people here who didn't especially want to get to know Steve any better in the near future. But I had to say something. So I blurted out the first thing that came into my head. "We aren't friends. He's my brother."

I didn't think it was all that funny but both Mary and Steve burst out laughing at the same instant. Then Steve stepped forward and held out his hand. "My name's Steve, ma'am," he said. Ma'am? I thought as they shook hands. Get real, Steve. When was the last time you called somebody ma'am?

But, I had to admit, it worked on Mary. I could see Steve had her impressed — or fooled, depending on how you looked at it.

Right about then it occurred to me that Steve and I should be getting home. Pop would be wondering where we'd got to — if he'd missed us yet. I gave Steve a nudge. "Hey, it's gettin' late," I said, hoping he could take the hint.

He glanced at his watch, grinned, and then turned dead serious. "Yeah, Beau, it's almost eleven. Past your bedtime. Let's get goin'."

The next thing I knew, he was heading for the car and I was standing there like a fool and feeling my ears getting red.

"Thanks for everything, Steve," Mary called to his disappearing back. "We all really appreciate you showing up just when we needed you."

I caught a glimpse of Raine's face just as Mary said that. Wrong, Mary, I thought. There's at least one person who didn't appreciate my brother showing up at all. The thought gave me a lot of satisfaction.

Five

I kept quiet for about half the way home. Then my curiosity got the best of me. "Steve?" I said.
"Yeah?"
"You lied to me about Vancouver, didn't you?"
He turned toward me, his face lit by the glow of the instrument panel. For once there was no trace of a smile. "What makes you think I was lying?"
"Figure it out. You don't spend all those years hanging out on some beach in Vancouver and then walk in here and handle a horse the way you did. You've been working with horses."
He shook his head and laughed softly. "That's what you think I've been doing all the time out there? Hanging out on the beach? You ever been to Vancouver?"
I shook my head. "Pop's not real big on trips these days. Especially not to cities. His idea of a major holiday was when we took a saddle to a guy up at Lloydminster and stayed overnight for the rodeo."
Steve laughed. "Yeah, I guess Pop always was kinda like that."

There was a pause. Then he went on. "Vancouver isn't all Stanley Park and English Bay, you know."

Actually, I *didn't* know, but I kept quiet and didn't advertise my ignorance.

Steve finally got to the point. "I worked for a guy who had a stable out there for a while."

"Yeah?" I said. "What kind of horses?"

"Thoroughbreds. Race horses. I used to exercise them at first. Worked my way up to training some. Did a little jockeying on some 'B Circuit' tracks for two or three years." Then, his voice going kind of quiet, almost like he was talking to himself, he added, "Working with horses was the only thing I ever did that made any sense."

I gave him a puzzled look "So if you liked the job so much, why'd you quit? You get too big for jockeying?"

"No," Steve said, his eyes on the road. "I didn't get too big. I got too smart."

Before I could ask what that was supposed to mean, we were pulling into the yard. The house was dark. Even having his oldest son home for the first time in seven years hadn't kept Pop up past eleven. But, I reminded myself, Steve hadn't exactly spent the evening hanging around reminiscing with Pop either.

I had to convince Steve all over again that I didn't mind sharing the bed but we finally got settled down and just lay there for a while in the semi-dark, not saying anything. I wondered what Steve was thinking, if he was going back in time like I was, remembering the room we shared upstairs in the old house on the ranch. We would have been laughing and talking up there in the dark, whispering so Pop wouldn't hear us and yell from the bottom of the stairs for us to shut up and go to sleep. But things were different then. In those days, Steve and I were really close.

-) Now I didn't know what to say. There was too much empty time between us. Too much I wanted to know but couldn't ask. Steve was right beside me now, so close I could feel his breathing, but it still felt like he was five hundred miles away.

He yawned. "That Rebel is some horse," he said sleepily.

"Yeah, you and him really hit it off." I paused for a yawn of my own. "You always did get along better with horses than people."

He shifted his head to look at me. "What was I supposed to do? Salute whenever J.C. barked? He's a phoney. All he knows about horses is how much he paid for 'em."

"I wasn't talking about J.C."

Steve laughed. "Oh, you mean Thunderstorm."

"Her name's Raine," I said sourly.

"Close enough. Any way you look at it, she's a long stretch of bad weather. She's a spoiled brat. Daddy's little girl. Anything she wants she gets. She thinks she owns the world."

"She's not like that!" I said, suddenly wide awake and half sitting up to face my brother. "She was just upset about Donovan and Rebel, and then you had to go and get on the wrong side of her."

Steve sat up too. "No kiddin' I got on the wrong side of her. If she'd hit me any harder I'd need new teeth." He was grinning in the moonlight, refusing to take me seriously.

"Okay, okay. You don't have to like her. But at least you've gotta admit she's one great-lookin' girl."

There was a long silence, so long I didn't think he was going to answer me at all. Slowly, the smile faded from his face. "Yeah, Beau," he said at last, in a voice grown strangely tired and far away, "she's good-lookin', all right. She looks a lot like someone I used to know."

That wasn't the kind of statement to just end there. I waited for him to go on, to tell me about the girl, who-ever she was. I could have waited forever. The silence grew. Then Steve turned toward me, and just for a second, our eyes met. It was like we were trying to see each other through a wall. Then he turned away and lay down. "Get some sleep, Beau," he said.

I sighed and lay down, facing the opposite direction. " Night, Steve," I said, for the first time since I was nine.

It seemed like I'd just closed my eyes when all of a sud-den, I was awake again. My watch, glowing in the dark, read 3:03. Usually, nothing short of an earthquake woke me before daylight. But something was different about tonight. Steve, I thought, hazily. That was it. My long-lost brother was here, sharing the bed with me — except that he wasn't. I was facing the wall, but even without moving, I could sense that the space beside me was empty. I turned over and saw that the room was silver with light from the full moon. Then I saw Steve. He was sitting on the bench by the window, his hands locked around his knees, his head leaned back against the wall, staring out into the night.

For a while I just lay there watching him silhouetted against the moonlit window. This was the first chance I'd had to really study him — without him being able to study me at the same time. Yeah, I thought, he did have the Garrett look all right. I would have known him if I'd been expecting him. The eyes were the real give-away, but the rest was there too — the stubborn chin, the little lines at the corner of his mouth . . .

You could tell we were brothers, all right. We came from the same mould — he just came out a little better. I was a not-bad-looking kid, but Steve had the kind of looks people never forgot.

Suddenly, a wave of anger flooded through me as I watched him there, spray-painted with moonlight, his face chiselled and perfect, the muscles of his shoulders sculpted like one of those old marble statues. So this is what you get, I thought. You break all the rules, run away at twelve, dump school, tear up what little's left of your family — and seven years later you come back, tall, cool, and handsome, driving a hot purple car. Yeah, Steve, you really messed up. How come they never put you in all those neat little "stay in school and make something of yourself" ads?

But then he shifted slightly and the moonlight fell stronger on his face. At first I couldn't believe what I was seeing. But when he wiped his hand across his cheek, smearing the wetness, I knew it was true. I had to make one addition to my brother's biography. Tall, cool, handsome, with a hot car — and a reason to be awake at three in the morning, crying silent tears in the moonlight.

I wondered if I'd ever know that reason — or if I even wanted to. Silently, I turned back toward the wall. I couldn't watch my big brother cry.

Six

I woke up to early morning sunlight — and a pillow bouncing off my face. "You gonna sleep all day or what, Beau*regard*?" Steve's voice leaned slow and heavy on the last two syllables.

Instantly I was fully, and furiously, awake. Nobody called me Beauregard. Steve and Pop were probably the only two people in Fenton who even knew that was my full name and I was planning on keeping it that way.

Pop was born in Texas and I got named for his all-time favorite hero, General Pierre Beauregard — *Confederate* General Beauregard, which just goes to show the knack he's always had for picking losers.

Fortunately the name got shortened to Beau before I hit school or I'd have been a better fighter than the boy named Sue. As it was I didn't have too much trouble — except that nobody ever spelled Beau right — until last year, that is, when we started taking French and everybody in class found out my name meant "beautiful." I had a few fights last year . . .

And I was just about to have another one. I made

a flying leap at Steve's laughing face, he dodged, and I landed on the floor, taking all the blankets with me. I grabbed Steve's foot and tripped him and he landed on top of me. We started wrestling and all of a sudden it was like Steve had never been gone, it felt so natural to be tearing up the house with him again. And I soon discovered that something else hadn't changed — the age gap between us. I might have been a whole lot bigger and stronger than the last time we did this but Steve was still three years older than me and the difference showed. Next thing I knew he had me down and was twisting my arm. "Say uncle," he ordered. I gritted my teeth and didn't say anything, and all of a sudden the pressure was released.

"Yeah, that's right." Steve laughed and gave me a friendly slap on the shoulder as he let go of my arm. "You never would say that unless I nearly killed you." Before I could say anything he rolled over on his stomach and propped his right elbow on the floor. "Okay, arm wrestle," he challenged.

"You'll be sorry," I said, kicking loose from the tangled blankets and lining up head to head with him. I gripped his hand.

"Okay, go for it," he said, and our arm muscles went rigid.

It was close, the closest I'd ever come to beating my brother. We must have lain there for over five minutes, puffing and sweating and turning red but neither of us giving an inch. Then, a little at a time, I felt the pressure begin to increase and slowly, a fraction of an inch at a time, he forced my hand downward. Finally I gave in. The back of my hand touched the floor and Steve let go with a sigh of relief. We lay there massaging our aching wrists and laughing. "Tell you one thing, baby brother,'' Steve said, "I'm glad I came home *this* year. Next year you would've beat me.''

Suddenly he switched hands. "Now left-handed,'' he said.

"Okay, you're on,'' I agreed. Too late, I caught the wicked laughter in his eyes.

"Oh, no,'' I groaned as our hands locked. You never gave Steve a left-handed chance at anything if you could help it. Not when he'd been a southpaw all his life. I can still see Pop going crazy trying to teach him to rope. He always did everything backwards.

And in school — maybe that was one reason he had so much trouble. That unreadable scrawl of his that he wrote with his hand turned around at an impossible angle like he was trying to stab himself in the heart with the pen.

Billy the Kid. That's how I used to think about my brother when I was little. The left-handed gunfighter — even though I found out later that old Billy probably wasn't left-handed at all.

"Come on, Beau, concentrate,'' Steve ordered, "you're makin' this too easy.'' I concentrated — on the fact that my knuckles were already brushing the floor.

I shook my head. "Billy the Kid,'' I said between breaths as I made one futile, last-ditch effort to force his hand up. Steve laughed and I knew he remembered too.

"Yeah,'' he said slowly. "Guess I was born to be an outlaw.'' He was smiling but his eyes were suddenly shadowed by some deep-buried pain that took me back to the moonlit scene in the middle of last night. Now I was sure I hadn't dreamed it.

I always wondered if Steve might have said more if Pop hadn't walked in right then. Well, not really in.

Between me and Steve and the blankets and pillows there wasn't much floor space left. Pop leaned on the doorframe, his greying hair uncombed, and surveyed the scene with something between disgust and interest.

"Mornin', Pop," I said. "We were, uh, wrestling."

"No kiddin'," Pop said. "Could've fooled me. I'd have swore we'd had another of them famous Alberta tornadoes." He took another look around the room and shook his head. "Well, breakfast'll be ready in about five minutes, which time you two jackrabbits better use to get this place halfway livable again." He started to turn away but then shot a parting glance at Steve, still sprawled in the middle of the floor. "Sure a good thing you showed up," he said. "Your kid brother needed somebody to teach him to act like an adult." He headed off down the hall and I could tell by the sound of his footsteps that his knee was acting up again.

Steve propped his chin on his hand and gave me a puzzled look. "Is he really mad?" he asked.

"Naw, that's about as cheerful as he gets."

Steve got up and started throwing the bed back together. "Yeah," he said thoughtfully, his back toward me. "I guess Pop's had some bad times."

Well, Steve, I thought as I got up and grabbed the other corner of the blanket he was straightening, you ought to know. You were the cause of the worst of them. What kind of a time did you expect him to have when you just disappeared on him when you were twelve, leaving him not knowing if you were alive or dead?

I might have gotten around to saying it out loud, but at that instant, a small dark hurricane came skidding around the corner, all four studded tires clawing for traction. It vaulted from the doorway to the bed in one flying leap and ended up as a lump under the blanket.

Steve just stood there, eyeing it in disbelief for a couple

of long seconds. Then, very slowly, he turned to me. "Beau," he said. "I have never seen anything quite like that before when I've been sober. What kind of an extra-terrestrial's under there?"

I laughed. "That," I said, "is Willie. If you want to get to know him better, run your hand in there under the blanket. Use your right. That way you'll still be able to eat after the amputation."

Looking like Indiana Jones about to enter the Temple of Doom, Steve reached his hand — the left one — under the corner of the blanket. Instantly, the lump turned into a streak of lightning that tore a long tunnel all the way across the bed and . . .

"Ouch!" Steve yelled, jerking out a bleeding finger. One dainty, black-barred paw with four curved daggers on the end also came out, explored the air, and retreated to become part of the lump again.

Steve sucked the blood off his finger and stared, fascinated, at the lump. Then, very carefully, he reached under the blanket again. And Willie got him again. Steve wiped his hand on his jeans. "That little sucker is *fast*," he said admiringly, and right then I knew that Willie had my brother hooked — in more ways than one — and that breakfast would have to wait until the game was over.

It took a while, but finally Steve reached in — with a hand that looked like it had been attacked by a rabid barbed-wire fence — and brought out a ball of dark fur that stared up at him out of innocent ice-green eyes and started to purr. Steve returned the look. "You are one b-a-a-d cat, Willie," he announced solemnly. Willie took that for a compliment and purred in overdrive. "But you don't look like a Willie to me. That's a dumb name for a cat. You oughta be a Billy cat."

"Tell Pop," I said. "He named Willy and there's another one he called Waylon."

Steve groaned. "How'd Pop end up with a *pair* of cats?"

"Somebody dropped 'em off at the gate last winter. Pop growled around for about a week about how he wasn't gonna be a nursemaid for any cats and how he supposed he'd have to shoot the pair of them."

"Don't look like he ever got around to it," Steve said, scratching Willie under the chin.

"The cats kinda talked him out of it. First he started feeding them. Then it turned real cold and he decided they could sleep in the house — just in the basement, of course. And then, a couple of days after that, Waylon started sleeping on Pop's bed and next thing I knew they had names and dishes under the kitchen table."

Steve grinned. "Pop never was as tough as he thought he was.".

All of a sudden there was a bellow from the kitchen. "Well," Steve corrected himself fast, "not unless he's kept waiting for breakfast. Race you down there!" he yelled, taking off down the hall with Willie/Billy riding his shoulder like a witch's cat on a broom.

This time, I won.

Seven

Breakfast was good. Pop can cook when he puts his mind to it and I guess he must have put his mind to it that day. We all ate plenty but nobody said much. I didn't have time to say much, since I had to be at work by eight o'clock and I was going to be late.

"Pop?" I mumbled through a mouthful of pancake. "Can I borrow the truck to take to Kincade's today?"

Pop's usually pretty good about that. Details like me not having a driver's licence don't usually worry him too much.

But this time he shook his head. "Sorry, Beau. I'm heading for Pincher Creek in about ten minutes. Promised Pete I'd have his saddle down there by noon."

I'd forgotten all about the saddle. Well, that took care of me getting the truck all right. "But I'll drop you off when I leave if that's not too late," he said.

Before I could answer, Steve spoke up. "Never mind, Pop. I ain't real busy. I'll give him a ride."

"Okay," Pop said, and that was that. Nobody asked my opinion again. Then it occurred to me that having my big brother around suddenly turned me into being the "little brother" again. I wasn't entirely impressed.

I was even less impressed when Pop suddenly checked his watch, got up and grabbed his jacket. "You all stay out of trouble today," he said, and headed for the door. It wasn't till I looked out the window and saw him loading the saddle in the truck that I realized that had been goodbye. The next thing I knew, he was driving out of the yard — leaving behind a kitchenful of dirty dishes again.

I filled the sink and cleared off the table, trying not to stumble over Steve, who was still sitting there drinking coffee like he had all day to waste — which, come to think of it, he probably did.

"Welcome to the family," I said, tossing the dish rag at him. "Your turn to wash."

"You've gotta be kiddin'," he said, eyeing the dish rag like it was contagious.

I wasn't kidding. He washed. It was not a pretty sight. I sent the frypan back to him three times before it was clean enough to dry — and I'm not exactly Betty Crocker in the kitchen myself.

By the time we finally got down to the Quarter Circle I was nearly twenty minutes late for work. J.C. wasn't going to be happy.

Steve pulled the Dodge up in front of the house and I jumped out. "Thanks for the ride," I said — and then realized he was getting out too. "Where you going?" I asked kind of nervously. Having Steve hang around here irritating J.C. — not to mention Raine —definitely wasn't part of the plan.

He shrugged. "Thought I'd say hello to a friend of mine," he said. What I was thinking must have showed on my face, I guess, because suddenly he laughed. "The horse, Beau. I just want to see how his leg is and then I'm outa here, okay?''

Before I could answer, the door of the house opened and Raine came out. "Hey!" I yelled, teasing her. "I thought *I* was late. How come you're just comin' out? J.C. goin' soft or something?''

Raine stopped, stood still, and gave me a strange look. "J.C.'s not here," she said in a small voice.

"What?''

"He's in the hospital in Calgary. He had a heart attack last night.''

The words echoed in a deep well of silence. I knew I should say something, but for a minute I just stood staring at her, afraid to ask the question that was on my mind. Finally I blurted it out. "Geez, Raine, I'm sorry. But he's gonna be okay, isn't he?''

There was another silence that seemed to last forever. Raine swallowed hard. "I guess so," she said at last, her voice kind of hoarse and uneven. "Mom went with him in the ambulance. She phoned back and said the doctor told her he was out of danger for the present, whatever that means.''

She stepped out of the shadow of the house and I got my first good look at her face. I knew then that she'd been crying. "You've been here by yourself all night?" I said, suddenly feeling like I wanted to protect her from all the pain in the world — especially the pain in her world. "Why didn't you call me?''

She raised her head and a little of the spark came back into her eyes. "Why? You think I need a babysitter?" Then her voice softened. "There wasn't anything you could do, Beau. No point in you being awake all night too.'' She managed a weak smile. "Somebody's gotta be able to work today. We're short-handed enough with both Dad and Donovan gone. We'd better get started on the chores.''

She wiped her shirt sleeve across her eyes, straightened her shoulders, and headed for the barn. That was Raine for you. When things got tough, so did she. I fell into step beside her and noticed that Steve did too. He didn't say anything to her but I saw the look he gave her. This time I thought there might be a trace of respect in it.

We went to check Rebel first. He was still favoring the right front leg quite a bit but Steve checked the cut and said it looked good. He put the halter on him and started to lead him outside. "What do you think you're doing?" Raine demanded.

"Taking him out for some exercise."

"He can hardly put any weight on that leg. He needs rest, not exercise."

"If he stands still too much it'll stiffen up on him," Steve said, leading the horse past Raine and on outside.

Raine followed. "Is there anything around here you *don't* know?" she demanded.

Steve shrugged. "Sure," he said, nodding toward the hayfield over behind the barn. "I don't know what you're planning to do about those cows."

"What cows?"

"The ones in that field over there using those round bales for bowling balls."

"What?" Raine swung around to follow the direction of Steve's gaze and I climbed up on the corral fence to get a better look. I was just in time to see Chester, the big old Simmental bull, tackle one of those thousand-pound bales, sending it rolling across the field, and giving a whole new meaning to the word "bulldozer." The whole field was full of cows, happily tearing mouthfuls of hay out of the bales, all playing their own version of "if you don't eat it, wreck it."

Raine muttered something under her breath that J.C. would have considered unladylike. "Dad said that fence was getting bad," she added, her voice tight. "He was going to start rebuilding it today. And now . . ." The words trailed off.

"And now," I added, trying to cheer her up, "we better get those cows out of there before they finish breakfast and start on dinner. Come on, Steve, let's see if you can outrun a cow."

From the look my brother gave me, I don't think the idea really appealed to him, but before he could say anything Raine spoke up. "Never mind, Beau. I'll get Fox. It'll be faster in the long run with a horse."

A couple of minutes later she came out of the barn leading Fox. She swung into the saddle and headed out across the field, riding hell-bent-for-leather as usual. I always had to smile when I looked at Raine riding Fox. The two of them were about as much alike as human and horse could get. Like right now, Raine bent low over Fox's neck, her long, strawberry-blond hair almost tangling with Fox's wind-whipped red-gold mane, riding with that perfect balance of hers, always moving exactly with the horse.

Steve gave a low whistle as he watched her sweep through the field and send the cattle galloping back out through the hole they'd made in the fence. "Well," he said, "I'll give the rich girl credit for one thing. She can ride."

I gave him a nasty look. "You bet she can ride," I said. "And quit calling her that."

Steve just raised an eyebrow and grinned, but I'd had about all the joy of brotherhood I could stand for a while. "Haven't you gone home yet?" I said through my teeth and I think I would have said some more if Raine hadn't called me just then.

She was off the horse, inspecting the hole where the cows had gone through the fence. I went over to have a look. Actually, you could hardly call it a hole in the fence. It was more like a hole with a little bit of fence in *it*. Raine surveyed the damage and shook her head. "Well," she said. "Looks like we'll be fencing the rest of the day."

Steve wandered up, laid a hand on one of the still-standing fence posts and wobbled it back and forth a little. It broke off just above the ground. "You know," he said thoughtfully. "This whole fence needs rebuilding. If we fix this up those cows will probably just break in on the other side. Maybe it would be smarter to leave the fence for now and haul the bales off the field."

Raine gave him a narrow-eyed look. Then, kind of reluctantly, she nodded. "Yeah," she said, "Dad was going to let the cows in here as soon as we got the hay moved anyway."

"You got a truck with a bale handler on it?"

"Of course we do."

"Don't suppose you know how to run it without breaking something," Steve said.

"Yeah, Steve, I know how to run it without breaking something," Raine echoed, her voice catching the same mocking tone as his.

He just laughed. "In that case you better get started."

Raine smiled, a dangerous sign. "Good idea, Steve. And if you're gonna hang around here all day you might as well get started too."

"Doing what?"

Raine nodded toward the far end of the field.

"There's five hundred square bales down there at the other end. *They* have to be loaded on the wagon by hand, unloaded, and stacked. Since I'll be busy with the round ones I guess you guys will have to take care of those."

⇀Next thing I knew she was in the saddle and heading for the barn at a dead gallop. I looked at all those bales waiting out there in the hot sun. I looked at my hotshot brother with his big mouth.

If today was going to be the first day of the rest of my life, it was one heck of a way to start.

"I hope you can work half as good as you can talk," I muttered as we walked over to the shed to get the tractor and wagon.

"Just try and keep up, little brother," Steve said.

I was just about to start the tractor when Raine hollered at me from over by the bale truck. "Beau?"

"Yeah?"

"You seen the truck keys?"

"No, aren't they in it?"

"No, maybe they're in the house. I'll check." She'd only walked a few steps when she stopped. "Oh, great," she muttered.

"What's wrong?"

"I just remembered where the keys are. I saw Dad put them in his jeans pocket last night."

"And he had those same jeans on when they took him to the hospital?" I said.

Raine sighed. "You got it, Beau. The keys are in Calgary."

"What about the spare set? Do you know where it is?"

She nodded. "Yup," she said, "I know where it is. Donovan always kept one set in *his* pocket."

"Oh," I said.

"Well," Raine said, "I guess we fix the fence after all."

Steve had wandered over just in time to throw in his two bits' worth. "That's gonna waste a lot of time."

That wasn't what Raine needed to hear right then. "No kiddin'," she snapped. "And I suppose you've got a better idea, as usual."

"Yeah," Steve said. He got in the truck and closed the door. I saw him dig something out of the toolbox on the seat and then his head disappeared out of sight under the dash for a minute. Suddenly the engine roared to life.

Steve jumped out of the truck, checked his watch, and grinned. "Beat my old record by eight seconds," he announced.

Raine stared at him like he was half a worm she'd just discovered in an apple she was eating. "You hot-wired it!" she said accusingly.

"No kiddin'? You're pretty smart for a girl." Still grinning, Steve leaned back against the fender and lit a cigarette.

Raine was furious. "So is that what you did for a living back wherever you came from? Ripped off cars? Is that how you got that purple pansy you drive?"

Steve took a drag on his cigarette before he got around to answering. "Sure, Raine," he said coolly, "all the time. You didn't think I was dumb enough to work for a living, did you? Just for the record, though, the car was bought legal." He paused, and his grin turned wicked. "But I can pick you up a stereo for this wreck next time I'm in town if you want."

"No thanks, Steve," Raine shot back, her voice sizzling with contempt. "I get things the old-fashioned way — by paying for them."

"Oh yeah, that's right, I keep forgetting. You *own*

this place, don't you, rich girl? You can buy anything you want, people included.''

Raine took a step forward. 'Don't you call me that! At least I'm not a sleazy two-bit punk who comes cruising in here and . . .''

Right then I lost my temper. Not because of what Raine was saying about my brother. I figured that was most likely true. But I'd just had enough of listening to the two of them stand around and snarl at each other like a couple of cats trying to get up nerve enough to get on with the fighting. ''All right!'' I yelled, slamming my fist on the hood of the truck so hard I almost said ''Ouch!'' and spoiled the whole effect. ''Knock it off, you guys! Let's either get this job done or forget the whole thing and I'll go home.''

There was instant silence as they both turned to stare at me like I'd just pulled a gun or something. I guess I don't get riled very often, so when I do it's kind of a tourist attraction.

Suddenly Steve started to laugh. ''All right, Beauregard!'' he said admiringly. ''Let's go to work.'' He turned and started walking toward the tractor, but then he stopped and looked back. ''So, lady,'' he said to Raine, ''you want me to unwire the truck or what?''

There was a silence during which Raine turned a nice shade of technicolor red. ''No,'' she muttered at last, refusing to meet Steve's eyes. ''I don't want you to unwire it. We need it to move the bales.''

Steve smiled. ''No kiddin','' he said.

Raine looked up, still red. ''And get rid of that cigarette before you get near that dry hay. That's a disgusting habit anyway.''

Steve studied the cigarette. ''I've had worse,'' he said softly. Then he shrugged and dropped the cigarette and ground it into the dust.

Eight

---

*I*f I never saw another bale of hay, it would be too soon. I reached that conclusion by about noon and we were still only half finished. It was a real hot day and there's no hotter job than handling hay. I wanted to take my shirt off but there's also no scratchier job than handling hay, so I left it on and suffered. Steve took his off — and suffered. In about an hour he was looking like he'd come down with a pretty good case of diaper rash — on his arms and chest. I noticed he was getting blisters on his hands too — which gave me a kind of secret satisfaction. There were some things that driving a hot car and playing rock guitar didn't get you in shape for. Plain old work was one of them.

But I had to admit that Steve *could* work. In spite of the scratches and blisters, he set a pace that was all I could do to match and he even seemed to be kind of enjoying it.

Raine finished hauling the round bales before we finished the square ones and came to give us a hand. Since all she'd done so far was drive the truck, she still had enough energy left to set a pace that kept both me and Steve sweating — and I could see that *she* was enjoying that too.

It was quarter to six when we finished the job and the three of us collapsed on the shady side of the porch, too tired to move, drinking ice-cold Coke and discovering aches in muscles we didn't even know we had.

Finally Steve stretched and stood up. "I'm starved. Anybody want to come to town for a pizza?"

Instantly I was on my feet. "You bet." I turned to Raine. "Come on, let's go."

She hesitated. "Come on," Steve said. "It's either that or your own cooking. And we already tried that."

He was talking about what had passed for lunch. A loaf of bread, a jar of peanut butter, a package of cheese, and a head of lettuce, all thrown in the middle of the table. Raine definitely threw bales better than she cooked.

Now she shot him a dirty look and I thought they were getting ready to start up again but then she laughed. "Yeah," she said a little sheepishly. "Guess you got a point there. You buying?"

"Not likely. We'll flip for it, fair and square. Odd man buys."

"Fair and square, huh? You should find that a new experience," Raine said, digging a quarter out of her pocket.

We flipped. Steve lost.

Half an hour later we were eating house specials in Delorino's in Fenton.

Steve and I ate like horses but I noticed that Raine didn't eat much at all. That worried me. Raine's never been famous for her ladylike appetite.

I touched her gently on the shoulder. "You worryin' about your dad?"

She nodded. "When you guys went home to have a shower I phoned the hospital. All I could get out of them was that old 'doing as well as can be expected' routine." She swallowed had, tried to smile. "I just wish I could see Dad myself."

"You can," I said.

"Yeah? How'm I gonna get there?"

"Same way you got here." I gave Steve a meaningful look which he chose to ignore. The silence lengthened. In a minute Raine's pride would take over and she'd refuse to have anything to do with the idea. Come on, Steve, I thought, you're such a big shot with your hot purple car. It wouldn't hurt you to offer to drive her down to see her dad.

"So, Steve," I said, "what you gonna do, drive us to Calgary or let me borrow your car?"

He laughed out loud at that. Then he shrugged, stood up, and threw a five-dollar tip on the table for the dopey waitress who'd been hanging around him like a wasp hovering over a rotten apple.

"Let's go," he said with a careless grin, but I could see he didn't really like the idea of going to the city. The cashier came to take the money. Steve dug in his pocket and came out with a roll of bills, sorted through them, and finally handed the cashier a one-hundred-dollar bill to pay the eighteen-dollar check. He didn't have much choice. The bills were all hundreds.

He was just putting the change away when Raine came back from the washroom. She hadn't seen the hundreds. I was glad.

The trip to Calgary was quiet. I guess Raine was thinking about her dad, Steve was probably still mad at me for trapping him into this trip — and I had enough on my mind to keep me quiet for a long time.

At the hospital, we found Mary pacing the hall out-side Intensive Care. She was looking kind of rough — about the way you'd expect a person who hadn't slept for thirty-six hours to look.

"Mom!" Raine yelled, in a voice I was pretty sure was too loud for a hospital, and Mary's face lit up as she turned and saw us standing there by the elevator. "Am I glad to see you!" she said, throwing her arms around Raine and giving her a big hug.

Then she turned to me and Steve. "And the Garrett boys," she said with a smile. That had kind of a weird sound to it. Kind of made us sound like outlaws, you know, like the James Brothers or something. It was strange to be classified with my brother after all these years. Whether I liked it or not was another question.

"So how's Dad?" Raine asked anxiously.

Mary sighed. "Well, the doctor says he's holding his own . . ."

"What's that supposed to mean?" Raine burst out. "That's no better than 'as well as can be expected.' Can't I at least see him?"

Mary checked her watch. "Not for a few minutes yet. The doctor's with him right now. Let's go wait in the cafeteria. I need a coffee. Come on, guys, I'm buying."

Over coffee, Mary told us what the doctors had said about J.C. He was out of immediate danger, whatever that meant. But the next two weeks were crucial. "So," Mary finished, "it looks like I'll be staying here for another two weeks anyway. I'm sorry to have to leave you with all this responsibility, Raine, but can you and Beau manage to keep up with the really necessary chores somehow? Never mind about working with the horses. I'll make arrangements to sell all but our saddle horses as soon as I can."

Raine's eyes went huge. "Sell? Mom, we can't sell.

None of the young horses are ready. They need at least another month or two of training. They won't go for half what they're worth . . ."

Mary nodded. "Honey, I know that. But there just isn't any choice. We don't have a trainer now anyway. And there's no way you and Beau can possibly keep up with the training and all the other work. Besides, school starts in less than two weeks."

"But I could skip . . ."

"Oh no, you couldn't." Mary's voice was firm. "If your dad found out I was letting you skip school to train horses, he'd never forgive me."

Her gaze shifted to me. I hadn't even opened my mouth but all those years of being a teacher had given Mary pretty good radar. "And don't you go getting any ideas, Beau. We've managed to keep you from escaping this long. I'm not about to let you quit in grade ten to train horses either."

Her voice sounded tired. "No, what we need is a full-time trainer that knows what he's doing, works cheap, and can start tomorrow. If I could find such an animal, I'd hire him today."

Raine just sat there, silent, staring into her empty cup. I knew how she must be feeling. More than anyone I ever knew, Raine lived and breathed horses. It didn't matter how hard the work was, how long the days were, or how dirty her hands got, she loved every minute she spent working with horses. Getting rid of them all now would break her heart. And from what I'd been able to take in about the shape of finances around the Quarter Circle, selling the colts untrained like that would probably be all it would take to break the ranch. And if the Kincades had to sell out . . .

Just thinking about it was giving *me* a hollow feeling in the pit of my stomach. I suddenly realized how much of my life was tied up with the Quarter Circle. It was more than just a job. I spent more time there than I did at home. Sometimes it _felt_ more like home than home did. There was always something interesting going on, Mary treated me like part of the family, and even J.C. wasn't so bad when you got used to him.

But most of all there was Raine. What if she moved away and I never got to see her again?

There had to be another way. I'd be willing to try anything to help her hang on to the horses. But when, all of a sudden, Raine came up with an answer, all I could do was stare at her. Slowly, she looked up, her chin set with a determination that made J.C.'s stubbornness seem downright obliging. I'd been the victim of that look before. Resisting it could be hazardous to your health. But she wasn't aiming it in my direction this time.

"Well," she said slowly, "I think I know where to get such an 'animal.' "

That's when I realized she was looking straight at Steve.

Raine wanted to hire _him_? I sat there about half stunned, trying to take in the idea. The way the two of them got along I figured she'd just as soon hire a cobra.

I looked at Mary to see what she was thinking, but from her puzzled expression I could see she hadn't figured out what Raine was talking about.

Then I looked at Steve. _He_ understood. But I couldn't figure his reaction. I thought he'd laugh at her. Helping out at the Quarter Circle for a day was one thing, but I didn't figure day-in, day-out ranch work was quite his style.

I should have known better than to try to figure Steve. He and Raine just looked at each other for a few long seconds. Then he asked softly, "Are you serious?"

Raine nodded. "I'm dead serious." There was a tone

to her voice I'd never heard before, almost pleading.

Steve shrugged. "Okay," he said carelessly. "I'll do it." Then he turned to Mary. "If your mom goes for the deal."

Mary sat up a little straighter, rubbed her forehead wearily, and focused on Steve. "I know I'm tired," she said, "but I didn't know I was *that* tired. What exactly did I just miss that I might or might not 'go for'?"

"I think the boss's daughter just hired me to train your horses," Steve said, a little crinkle at the corner of his mouth.

Raine met her mother's eyes. "He can do it, Mom. He stopped Rebel last night, remember? And he's already been working at the ranch all day today. Please, Mom. Let's at least try. If we hire him we'll have enough help to keep the horses."

She finally stopped long enough for Mary to get a word in edgewise. "Whoa," she said firmly, like she was disciplining a runaway colt. "Let's take this one step at a time. First of all I'd like to find out if Steve knows what he'd be getting into working at the Quarter Circle. There's a lot more to it than just working horses, you know. A lot of it's just plain farm work."

"Yeah," Steve said, inspecting a big blister on his hand. "I got educated about that today."

"The cows broke into the alfalfa field so we hauled all the bales off it," Raine explained.

"Not a bad day's work," Mary said thoughtfully. "And you're still willing to go back for more, Steve?"

Steve nodded. "I never was too bright," he said with a slow grin.

A hint of a matching grin crossed Mary's face but then she turned serious. "Well," she said, "obviously you're willing to work and what you did with Rebel was pretty impressive, but I need to know more than that . . ."

"I worked at a thoroughbred stable for a couple of years," Steve said. "I get along with horses. I don't know much about what your horses are being trained for but Raine and Beau can show me."

Mary was wavering. I figured her common sense was telling her to get on with selling those horses and get the whole business off her mind. But Mary and Raine had a lot in common. Sometimes they did what they felt instead of what they thought. "Well," she said. "You're finished school, then, are you Steve?"

"Yeah," Steve said, "I've been through with school for a long time."

Mary's forehead wrinkled with concentration and I could see her mental computer hard at work — and not getting any answers that made sense about that. But she let it go. "All right," she sighed. "We'll give it a try temporarily. If it works out till J.C.'s well enough to think about it, it'll be up to him from there on. Eight dollars an hour is the best I can offer you right now."

"Good enough," Steve said. Solemnly, he and Mary shook hands. I heard Raine breathe a big sigh of relief. And I just sat there wondering what all three of them had just gone and done.

Nine

A minute later Raine and Mary were gone to see J.C. That left me and Steve. For a while neither of us said anything. He got himself another coffee and sat there sipping it moodily and blowing smoke rings. I sat and watched him. Finally he looked over at me. "Got somethin' on your mind, Beauregard?"

"Yeah," I said, my voice taking on a hard edge. "Why are you doing this?"

He gave me a lazy look over the rim of his cup. "Doin' what?"

"Don't act any dumber than comes natural, Steve. Why are you getting yourself all set up with a job at the Quarter Circle?"

Steve set the cup down. "Figure it out, Beau," he said. "I need the job. Kincades need the help. That's not too complicated even for you."

"That's all there is to it, huh?"

"Should there be more?"

"I don't know," I said slowly, trying to see past that cool, arrogant smile of his. "All the pieces of you just don't fit together right somehow."

Steve laughed. "What's the matter, Beau? You think I'm in there to rip ol' J.C. off or something? Steal all his hay bales some dark night? Or take ol' Rebel and ride off into the sunset?" His eyes flashed wickedly. "Or maybe you're afraid it's the boss's daughter I'm out to steal, huh, Beau?"

It was my turn to laugh — but the laugh rang a little hollow. "Dream on, Steve," I said, the words coming out louder than I intended. "Raine hates your guts and you know it. She got Mary to hire you because you're available and because you happened to be in the right place at the right time with Rebel last night."

Steve just took another sip of coffee and let my words run off him.

"Look," I said, managing to lower the volume, "maybe you coming along right now is the best thing that could have happened to the Quarter Circle, or maybe it's the worst. I don't begin to understand what makes you tick. But I'll tell you one thing, Steve, if you do anything to hurt Raine — or her family — I'll make you pay."

Steve sighed. "Well, Beau," he said, sounding bored with the whole conversation, "I guess you're just gonna have to trust me."

Trust you, Steve? I thought. I might envy you. But trust you? Never.

Right then Raine came back in. "So how's your dad?" I asked.

"Grumpy as a bear in February," she said, making a face. I breathed a sigh of relief. However sick J.C. might be, at least his disposition was normal — and seeing him had left Raine relaxed enough to joke about it. "Come on," she said, heading for the door. "Let's get out of this place. Hospitals make me sick."

Ten minutes later we were headed up Highway 2. Raine was talking a blue streak, telling Steve everything about every horse on the Quarter Circle — right down to the color of their hoofs, I think. Steve, for once in his life, was being quiet and listening — and I was staring out the window, thinking.

We were getting close to Airdrie when Raine started explaining about a trick she'd been using to teach the sorrel filly to take the right lead. She was not only explaining, she was demonstrating, and she took a lot of room to do it. I shifted position to avoid getting her sharp elbow in the ribs again, and as I did, I suddenly caught a glimpse of the outside mirror. I swung around for a second look. No, I hadn't imagined it. A real colorful red and blue laser light show was going on behind us — and getting closer fast.

"Uh, Steve," I said, kind of casual, "how fast you goin'?" Still watching Raine's demonstration with one eye, he checked the speedometer. "'Bout 75. Why? Want me to go faster?"

"No, I, uh, think you better go slower. There's a cop wants you to pull over."

"What!" Steve checked the mirror, swore, and slammed his fist against the wheel.

I couldn't help laughing. Considering the way I'd seen him drive on the back roads, getting stopped for five miles over the speed limit now was pretty funny. "Take it easy, Steve," I said with a grin. "You can afford the ticket."

When he didn't answer me, I turned to look at him. In the greenish glow from the instrument panel, his face was set as hard as chiselled granite. I could see his knuckles, white from their grip on the steering wheel. Then, all of a sudden, he dropped the Dodge a gear and hit the gas. Engine roaring, the car leaped ahead like a quarter horse coming out of a starting gate.

A fist clenched in my stomach. "Steve," I said, amazed at the super-calm sound of my voice, "you don't want to do this."

I was wrong. He did want to do it. The car was still gaining speed. The light show behind seemed to be fading back a little as Steve pulled into the fast lane. We started passing cars. Somewhere behind us a siren started to howl. The cop car was in the passing lane too. The rest of the traffic might as well have not been there. It was just him and Steve . . .

But the other traffic *was* there. As the needle climbed past ninety I could see a knot of tail lights ahead. Traffic in all three lanes. We were bearing down on a car in the fast lane, its tail lights getting bigger and brighter with every second. Beside it, other cars cruised along, filling the right-hand lanes. The cop car was starting to gain on us.

Steve lay on the horn. I saw the driver ahead of us take a frantic look in his mirror, instinctively start to swing right, and just in time, remember the car to his right. I could see him hunch forward, leaning on the gas for all he was worth. I felt sorry for the guy. He was driving one of those little compact Chevy trucks like Pop's. That was probably all the speed he was going to get. Those things were too gutless to even catch bugs in the grill. Steve had the front end of the Dodge practically riding in the Chevy's box . . .

Newspaper headlines from last summer started flashing across my mind. SIX PEOPLE KILLED IN HIGH-SPEED CHASES. I remembered the worst one. Just a few more miles up this highway. Four people dead. I remember the pictures on the news. Unrecognizable clumps of metal that used to be cars . . .

A cold hollowncss startcd spreading through my insides. This was so stupid . . .

"Steve!" Panic was creeping around the edges of my voice. "For God's sake, slow down!"

Steve never even twitched. Eyes riveted on the car ahead and hands locked onto the steering wheel, he looked like he hadn't even heard me. But he had.

"Shut up, Beau," he said, low and cool like he was asking me what time it was. Then, "Hang on!" He jerked the wheel hard to the right. The car shuddered and suddenly lurched across the right lanes, headed for the ditch. I hoped dying didn't hurt too much . . .

The next thing I knew, the car was coming out of the skid, straightening out and clawing for traction some-where between the shoulder and the ditch. Then we were rocketing along the shoulder, slicing through the nar-row space between the car in the right lane and the ditch. We were so close to the other car that Steve and the saucer-eyed passenger could have reached out and touched each other.

Then we were past the car and swinging back, half out of control, into the driving lane. I looked back. The cop car was still in the fast lane, boxed in behind the struggling Chevy.

Airdrie was just ahead, the town right along the high-way — with plenty of cops real handy. I could see it all now. The cop behind us would radio ahead to the Airdrie cops. They'd be waiting ahead of us with the road blocked off, just like in all the movies. And then? And then, I didn't know. But I was pretty sure a roadblock wouldn't stop Steve.

Steve must have read that thought. "Gotta get off this

highway," he said, his voice low and tense. "Is there a back road that'll get us home?"

Before I could even think about it, Raine answered. "Take the Big Hill Springs road. Start slowing down now. It's the next exit."

I turned to stare at her in the darkness, wondering if her face was as calm as her voice. But all I could see was the dim outline of her face. It looked white.

Steve didn't slow down much. The next thing I knew, the exit sign was right in front of us and he was braking and wheeling the car through a squealing skid onto the turn-off. We took the corner so fast I had to grab the door handle to keep from sailing across the car. It reminded me of a midway ride I'd been on once at the Calgary Stampede.

The car straightened out and now we were heading west, into the night. There were no lights on this road, either coming toward us or behind us. And then Steve cut the lights on the Dodge too. For the first few seconds it was like being in a space ship, hurtling out of control through the huge, black emptiness of nowhere.

But this wasn't space. This was good old Alberta — where the deer and the antelope roam. And my mind kept painting me real colorful pictures of what would happen if one of them decided to roam across the road in front of us about now.

There was a little sliver of moon away up high and gradually my eyes adjusted so I could see the world in shades of black. The hardtop surface of the road ahead gleamed faintly. "The road was a ribbon of moonlight . . ." From out of nowhere, that line ran across my mind. Then I remembered where it came from. A poem we took in English last year. It was about this outlaw dude that tried to outfight the law — and the law won.

→I remembered other lines, from the end of the poem: "When they shot him down on the highway, / Down like a dog on the highway, / And he lay in his blood on the highway . . ."

I decided not to think of any more lines. I looked behind us instead — just in time to see the flashers of the cop car against the sky as the car topped a hill about a mile behind us.

Steve swore under his breath and I knew he'd seen it too. He started to speed up. "Slow down." Raine's voice was cool in the tension-filled air. "There's a gravel pit just over this hill on the left. Pull in there." Steve shot a glance in Raine's direction, then geared down as the gateway showed up ahead. There was a wire gate across the entrance — until the Dodge hit it and it snapped like a guitar string. A second later the car was crouched in the shelter of a huge pile of crushed gravel and we could hear the siren tearing a hole in the country-night silence, getting closer, closer . . .

In the next few seconds I found out what it was like to be a fox, holed up in your burrow and hearing the baying of the hounds. None of us breathed as the cop car came even with the gravel pit. I figured that with that busted gate lying there pointing us out, the cop couldn't miss. My nerves were humming as I waited for him to hit the brakes.

It didn't happen. I couldn't believe it. He was speeding up, his siren howling out behind him like he was even outrunning the sound. We sat there in dead silence. The flashing lights topped the next hill, hung silhouetted for a split second against the sky — and disappeared.

Steve took a deep breath and started the car. "He'll be back," he said, his voice low and tense. "And he'll bring all his friends. We've gotta find a back road goin' north."

We? I thought, furiously. *You* started this little game of hide and seek, Stevie boy. *You* find a road.

But before I could say it out loud, Raine spoke up. "There's a side road at the top of the hill going north. It'll connect with another that'll get us back to Fenton eventually."

I turned to stare at her, but down there out of the moonlight, I couldn't see her face. I knew Steve was looking at her too. "How do you know?" he asked.

"I lived around here till I was twelve," she said, her voice as cool as a spring rain. "Hurry up or that cop's going to be back."

We burned out of that gravel pit.

During the next hour Steve's shiny purple car got closely acquainted with every muddy gravel road in south-central Alberta. Steve muttered as we hit about the two-hundredth pothole but I just smiled. Except for the fact that I didn't really want to walk home, I would have laughed if the transmission fell out. I hadn't said a word to Steve since I'd got told to shut up back on the highway. An occasional "Turn left here" from Raine was the best it got for conversation the rest of the way home. I spent most of the time checking the mirror, expecting a phantom cop to light up the road behind us at any second.

We finally pulled into the Quarter Circle at 11:30. Steve cut the engine and wc all just sat there. It felt like the silence just before a thunderstorm breaks loose.

Steve was the first to move. Slowly, he let go of the wheel, took a deep breath, and turned to face Raine. "Look," he said, his voice tense, "I didn't mean for that to happen with you guys along." He looked away and his voice softened. "I couldn't help it."

Try again, Steve, I thought angrily, but I didn't say

anything. What I had to say could wait until we were alone. Anyway, it was Raine he was talking to, and she wouldn't even look at him. In the glow of the yard light her face was white and her jaw was set like a rock. She just kept staring straight ahead.

The silence stretched out. Steve broke it again, his voice rough. "You want me to say it for you, rich girl? Okay, I will. After what just happened you don't want me to show up for work here tomorrow. How's that? Did I get it right?"

Raine suddenly came to life. "No, Steve, you got it wrong," she said. "You got this job because we're desperate and you're all there is. And you've still got the job for the same reason. What you did tonight doesn't have anything to do with working on the ranch. But," she went on, in a voice edged in icicles, "the day you mess up in any way that *does* affect the Quarter Circle, you're gone. Got it?"

Steve met her look. He nodded. "Be pretty hard to miss it," he said. "See you in the mornin', boss."

"Let me out, Beau," Raine ordered in a tone that hadn't warmed up much.

Obediently I got out and held the door for her. Then I walked her to the house and waited while she dug through all her pockets twice before she finally found the key. Her hand wasn't completely steady as she put it in the lock. "Raine, are you sure you'll be okay here by yourself tonight?" I asked.

She tossed her head. "What do you suggest? Get the Garrett boys to babysit? No thanks!"

That was all it took. The anger that had been smouldering in me exploded into flames. "Hey," I said, my voice rising. "This is me, Beau. Remember? I didn't do anything. It wasn't me that decided to outrun the cops." I gave her a dirty glare. "I wasn't the one that was giving Steve directions on how to get away. Why'd you do it, anyway? I would've let him get caught. It would have served him right.''

Raine sighed impatiently and shook her head. ''Geez, Beau, when are you gonna grow up and use your head for something besides growing too much hair? After he tried outrunning them, the cops would have arrested him if they caught him. And where would that leave you and me? We're juveniles. They'd drag us down to the police station and call our parents.'' Her voice suddenly went tired. ''On top of everything else, my mom didn't need that.''

Before I could say anything she had stepped inside. ''Just go home, Beau,'' she said, and closed the door.

I stood there like an idiot, staring blankly at the door and wondering how my world had got so messed up. And I'd always thought that Raine really liked my hair.

Ten

Steve and I went home. We walked into the house together but if we'd been on different planets I couldn't have felt any farther away from him right then. I went in the kitchen, got the milk out, poured myself a glass, and put the milk back in the fridge. Steve walked over, took it out again, and poured himself a glass.

I sat down at the table and drank my milk, staring out the window and wishing my brother really *was* on a different planet. He sat down at the table, drank his milk, and stared at me. "You gonna sulk all night, or what, Beau?" he said at last.

I swung around to face him. "I'm not sulking. I just don't have anything to say to somebody who has to risk my girlfriend's life just to show off that his hot car can outrun the cops."

"I didn't do it to show off," he said, the challenge gone out of his voice.

"Yeah, sure Steve," I shot back, "then tell me why you did it?"

He shook his head. "I can't," he said.

Right then the phone rang. I picked it up. "Yeah?" I said. It was Pop.

"Well, hello to you, too, Sunshine," he said, sounding a lot more cheerful than he ever did at home. "You sound sour as a cat with his tail in the screen door. What's eatin' you?"

"Nothin'."

There was a pause. Then, "I tried to call you earlier. Where you been till this time of night?"

"Calgary. Raine wanted to go see J.C."

"Where's he?"

"In the hospital." I explained about what had happened.

Pop wasn't as surprised as I'd expected. "Poor ol' J.C.," he said. "He's been a heart attack waitin' to happen for as long as I can remember. How's he doin'?"

"Okay, I guess, but he'll be in there for a while." I wished he'd stop asking questions. He didn't.

"How'd you get to Calgary?"

"Steve," I said, and at that I caught a warning flash from my brother's eyes. What did he think? I was about to spill the whole story to Pop? He should know better than that. Even when we were little I never ratted on him. But I didn't mind making him sweat a little.

"And," I added, watching his face, "he decided to explore all the back roads so we were a long time getting back."

A voice told Pop to deposit more money and I could hear Pop mumbling something about American quarters. "Pop," I said, getting a sudden suspicion, "where are you?"

Silence. Then, "Well, I was just gettin' to that."

"Where, Pop?"

"Buffalo."

My mind did a speed search along its rarely used geography circuits. Only one answer came out. "Buffalo, New York?" I asked incredulously.

Pop gave a disgusted snort. "Don't they teach you anything in school? New York's a couple of thousand miles away. How'd you expect me to get there?"

"I didn't expect you to be anywhere except Pincher Creek. Buffalo, where?"

"Wyoming, of course. You've been there. I rodeoed there once when you were three. You sat on the big iron buffalo in front of the credit union. Remember?"

No, I didn't remember and I wasn't about to try. "What are you doing in Wyoming?"

"Well," Pop said thoughtfully, "it's a long story. I got to Pincher Creek just in time to give ol' Pete the saddle before he hit the road. And then he says, 'You know, Bob, I got a friend in San Antone that's been wantin' a custom-made saddle like this. I'm gonna head down there for a week or so after the show in Denver. Why don't you ride along with me, see some country, and maybe even make a little money while you're at it.' So —" Pop paused and then went on sounding just a little sheepish — "here I am."

So there he is, I thought. And here Steve and me are . . .

Pop was talking again. "I hope you don't mind too much, Beau. I know it's kinda sudden just takin' off like this but it ain't like you'll be all on your own. You got your brother to look out for you."

I almost had to shove my first in my mouth to keep from laughing. Try again, Pop, I thought. How about now I've got my brother to look out for, period.

"You still there, Beau?"

"Yeah."

"There's two hundred dollars in my dresser, under

my socks. That should keep you in groceries. The rent's paid up till the end of September. I'll call you in a few days and see how you're makin' out. Think you can manage?''

Well, Pop, I thought, Buffalo, Wyoming, is a little late to start asking. But then I thought about the excitement in his voice and I realized that for the first time since — since when? Since he quit rodeoing? Since he married Mom? — Pop was actually having fun.

"Sure, Pop," I said, trying to force a little enthusiasm into my voice. "No sweat. Have a good time down there."

"You bet, Beau!" Then his tone turned serious again. "Is Steve there?"

"Yeah."

"Let me talk to him."

I held the receiver out.

Slowly, almost reluctantly, Steve took it. "Yeah, Pop?"

He listened, his eyes on me. I had a feeling he wished I wasn't sitting there listening, but I wasn't about to miss this. A few seconds later, "No," he said. A pause, then, "No, I won't. It'll be all right." Another pause. "Relax, Pop. They won't. Not in Fenton." His face was expressionless.

I was getting real curious about what the other half of this conversation sounded like. There was a longer pause.

I watched as the muscles along Steve's jaw tightened a little. "Yeah, Pop, I'm sure. Everything's cool. No, I can't promise. I don't make promises. But I'll be careful."

Silence. Steve's face slowly relaxed. "Sure. Bye, Pop." He hung up the phone, stretched, and stood up.

"What was that all about?" I asked.

He just shrugged and flashed his arrogant grin. "Nothin', Beauregard. Just Pop makin' sure I was gonna stick around and babysit you till he gets back."

Liar, I thought. I might have said it out loud, but before I could he'd turned and was headed up the stairs. "I'll sleep in Pop's room tonight," he said over his shoulder.

Eleven

The next morning was weird. Steve was already in the kitchen making coffee when I got there. "Mornin', Beau," he said, real casual, like maybe last night had never happened.

I just looked at him, a lump of leftover anger sitting in my chest and blocking any words that might have come out. But I gave in. If we were going to live together, we'd have to talk to each other.

"Mornin'."

"Hand me your plate," he said. "I cooked breakfast." Before I could refuse, he'd scooped up two of the sorriest-looking little black and yellow objects I'd ever seen and slopped them onto my plate.

"Steve," I said slowly, "what are these?"

He gave me a disgusted look. "Fried eggs, stupid. What do they look like?"

I chose not to answer that question. Maybe they *had been* eggs but now even the hen that laid them would never have recognized them. I watched in awe as Steve shovelled his down. I drank some coffee, made some toast, and shoved the egg corpses around a little with my fork while I waited for an opportunity.

It came when Steve disappeared into the bathroom. I grabbed my plate and scraped the eggs into the cats' dish under the table. Sorry, guys, I thought, but anybody who eats mice complete with wrapping and stuffing must be hard to kill.

When we drove in at eight o'clock Raine was already half finished with the morning chores and she didn't waste any time getting us to work too. For me it was pretty much routine, all the same stuff I'd been doing all summer, only more of it. It was better, though, because I got to do some of the interesting stuff, actually teaching the horses something, instead of just doing the stable-hand jobs.

The first horse I worked was a young sorrel gelding named Arizona. I'd seen Russ Donovan ride him a few times before, and the colt had never so much as twitched, so I figured he was going to be one of those real easy horses that seem to be born about half broke. I was jogging Arizona in big slow circles around the corral when Steve brought Rebel out of the barn, put a longe line on him, and started him walking around the smaller corral. Raine was watching him. I could hear them talking but I couldn't make out the words. I wondered what was going to happen to Rebel with J.C. out of the picture for a while. One thing I'd bet on. Raine would never go along with the idea of selling him if she could help it.

Arizona tried slowing to a walk. I nudged him in the ribs. He shuffled back into a reluctant trot, hanging his head like an old plow horse. Not only was this horse naturally gentle, he was also naturally bone lazy. Training him was going to be about as exciting as watching the grass grow.

➜Steve had moved Rebel up to a trot. I tried to see if Rebel was still limping but the fence was in the way. Raine had moved closer to Steve and they were still talking quietly.

I couldn't believe they were getting along like that. All that electric aggravation that had sparked between them was gone. Now it was strictly business and they were both unbelievably polite to each other. It was like, since last night, there was a wall between them. I figured Raine had built it — but Steve was respecting it. Thinking it over, I decided I liked that arrangement fine. Now, if Raine would just try to remember that she and I were on the same side of that wall . . .

Arizona slipped into a walk again and I gave him an absent-minded jab with my heels. The next thing I knew, his head had disappeared somewhere between his front hoofs, his back hoofs were pointed at the sky and his back was arched like a bow about to send an arrow whizzing through the air. *I* was that arrow. By the time I realized he was actually going to buck, it was too late. I was too out of balance to ride him and I couldn't pull his head up fast enough to stop him. I made a perfect arc over his head, and landed in the dirt with an earth-shaking thud that knocked the wind right out of me for a second or two.

By the time I was breathing again and had my wits collected enough to look up, I realized I wasn't alone. Three heads were bent over, studying me with considerable interest. Raine, Steve — and, of course, good old Arizona.

"Are you all right, Beau?" Raine asked, trying hard not to laugh. The other two weren't even trying. Arizona blew through his nose at me with a little snort that I suspected was the horse equivalent of a giggle.

"Beau," Steve said, flashing his most wicked grin. "Did you, uh, mention something about taking up bronc riding?"

I ignored all three of them, creaked my way to my feet, and spit out a mouthful of dirt. "Somethin' must've spooked him," I muttered. "He started to unwind all of a sudden, before I had a chance to get ready."

Raine and Steve nodded solemnly. So solemnly I expected them to burst out laughing any second. Then, suddenly, a strange look crossed Raine's face. "Oh, no. I just realized that I never got around to telling you, Beau."

I gave my head a little shake. Either I'd sustained brain damage or this girl wasn't making any sense. "Tell me what?"

"Well," she said, looking a little sheepish — and at the same time trying to swallow a giggle. "Remember we were talking about the Fenton rodeo next week?"

"Yeah."

"I meant to tell you yesterday but I completely forgot . . ."

"*What*, Raine?"

"I phoned my entry in for the barrel racing."

I nodded, not understanding what made this such a big deal. "You said you were going to."

"Yeah," she said, a little hesitantly. "And I entered you in the novice saddle bronc."

"You *what*?"

"Well, you've been talking about doing it all summer. So now it's done." Her grey eyes studied my face. "Hey, Beau, if you don't want to do it, it's okay. I'll call back and get them to scratch your name."

I bent down, dusted off my pant leg, and tried to think. Yeah, I wanted to try the novice saddle bronc. I'd done okay at high school rodeos, even picked up a couple of trophy buckles. I was ready to give the Fenton rodeo a shot. I just hadn't figured on having my brother there to see it — especially not after the performance he'd just seen.

"Hey, don't do that, Raine," I said with a confident grin. "I wouldn't miss this chance for anything."

Steve gave me a slap on the shoulder. "I wouldn't miss it either, Beau."

I got back on Arizona — carefully, expecting he was probably so pleased with his first attempt at bucking that he'd want to try it again. He didn't. He just slopped around the corral, looking half-asleep again. I guess he and I had come to one of those unspoken deals horses and riders have been known to make. He wasn't going to dump me again — and I was going to pay attention to my own business while I rode him.

Twelve

---

*F*or the next few days, I worked harder than I'd ever worked in my life. I think all three of us did. When we weren't working horses we were fixing fence and hauling more bales. Eight-to-five workdays didn't exist any more. Most days we worked till dark. None of us took the weekend off either. As far as I was concerned, I'd rather be there with Raine than anywhere else. And Steve just shrugged and said he didn't have anything else to do right now and kept on working.

Every once in a while I'd catch myself staring at him, trying to figure him out. It seemed like a part of him, the cool city part, was laughing at everything my life was all about — me wanting to be a bronc rider like Pop, the way I felt about Raine, even Fenton. Since the night we'd stopped there for pizza he'd never even been back to town.

But then I'd watch him with the horses and realize all over again that what he'd done with Rebel that first night hadn't been luck. Steve was better with horses than anybody I'd ever seen. The ones he'd been working with for a few days already showed more training than Russ Donovan had put on them since early spring.

Donovan had figured he was the trainer and shouldn't have to get his hands dirty on ordinary chores, but Steve did more than his share of plain hard work. I watched him out by the alfalfa field one afternoon when the sun was hot enough to fry eggs. He was pounding fence posts by hand in a spot too rough to get the tractor and pounder in. Swinging that big, heavy post mall is about the hardest work there is and he was soaked with sweat and breathing like a wind-broke racehorse. But I'd never seen him look happier.

We never talked. I don't mean it like we weren't speaking to each other. We talked about the horses and the stuff we were working on at the Quarter Circle. We even had some pretty good laughs together — like the morning at breakfast when Willie spotted a fly buzzing on the window, jumped on the table to try and catch it, stepped on a plastic bread bag at the edge of the table, slipped and fell on top of Waylon, who was sunning himself on the floor — and set off the cat fight of the century under the kitchen table.

But we never talked about anything that mattered. Steve had been home a week and I didn't know any more about him than I did the night he walked up to the kitchen door. No, I *did* know more. I knew he had a pocket full of money and a deathly fear of cops — two things I wished I'd never found out.

On Wednesday, Mary came out from Calgary to see how things were going. I could see she was impressed. I was impressed too, because she cooked us a couple of meals. It was the first decent food I'd had all week — *and* I didn't have to cook it. I'd been cooking both dinner and supper most of the time lately. No, I *can't* cook. But at least what I made was nontoxic and biodegradable, which was more than I could say for Raine's or my brother's efforts.

J.C. was still in Intensive Care, but according to Mary, he was holding his own and grumpy as all-get-out. When Mary got ready to head back to the city Wednesday night, Raine decided to go along and stay down there overnight. "That's a great idea, Raine," Mary said, while we were eating supper. "It'll do your dad good to see you again. But how are you going to get home in the morning?" She paused, and automatically, she glanced in Steve's direction. I could read her mind. Steve had driven Raine to Calgary once; now he was actually on the ranch payroll and doing a great job, so naturally he wouldn't mind running down to pick her up in the morning. For the first time, I actually saw Steve lose some of that arrogant cool of his. He looked down at his plate and became deeply involved with pushing his meat loaf around with his fork.

I glanced at Raine. She was looking faintly pink and real uncomfortable. "I can get a ride to Fenton with Jim Gibson when he brings the freight up from the city in the morning," she blurted out. "I'll phone him right now." She went galloping off to the phone, leaving Mary sitting there with a puzzled little wrinkle between her eyes.

On Friday we started work at daylight and had the real necessary stuff done by noon. Then we loaded up my saddle — Pop's saddle, actually, the one he'd been letting me use since I started riding in high school rodeos — and Raine's horse and headed for the Fenton rodeo. All three of us. For a while there I thought — make that hoped — that Steve wouldn't come. He kidded Raine so much about what a Mickey Mouse sport barrel racing was that war just about broke out between them again, and I knew he wasn't about to let me forget that little bronc-riding exhibition that Arizona and I had put on.

Of course, there was the minor matter of who was going to drive to the rodeo grounds, but Raine and I decided that since it was only a ten-minute drive and we didn't have to go through town, there wasn't much chance of getting stopped. We flipped a coin to see which one of us would drive. She won.

All the time we'd been loading Fox, Steve had been over in the corral fussing with Rebel and ignoring us completely. We were finally ready to go. I was sitting sideways, leaning against the passenger door — unfortunately there was a big pile of tack and stuff between me and Raine — when, all of a sudden, the door opened and I almost fell out. "Move over, little brother," Steve said with a mocking grin. "You didn't think I was going to miss your moment of glory, did you?"

The barrel racing was one of the first events in the afternoon performance, so by the time we got Fox unloaded a bunch of the girls were already out in the arena warming up their horses. Raine swung into the saddle. "Wish me luck, Beau!" she said as she galloped away.

Steve and I wandered up by the fence and watched the girls — watched them practice, I mean. Fox had already worked herself into a sweat without even doing anything. She was tossing her head up and down, fighting the bit, wanting to get on with the run. "Crazy horse," I muttered. "She always starts tossing her head when she doesn't get her own way."

Steve gave me a sideways look. "Probably caught the

habit from her rider,'' he said, keeping his face dead serious.

I flashed him a dirty look, which he didn't notice. The barrel race was starting.

There were a lot of entries — ten or more — and I recognized some of the names as real serious racers that had been following the rodeo circuit all summer. Most of them had expensive horses, a lot of them bought already trained. I knew Raine wasn't counting on beating too many of them but I hoped she'd at least give them a run for their money.

The first three runs were good ones, between 17.5 and 18 seconds, but nothing too spectacular. Then a flashy-looking palomino with an equally flashy rider in a tight red jumpsuit came streaking across the arena. That horse was fast. The crowd roared as she took the first turn so tight the rider had to reach down and steady the barrel as they came around it. The second turn was perfect. And the third. The palomino stretched out for home like a golden arrow. Her time was 17.2 seconds. I shook my head. That was one Raine wasn't going to beat.

The next rider knocked over a barrel, collecting an automatic five-second penalty. Then a girl came in on a big bay that was obviously just learning the business. He could run fast enough, but a Mack truck could have turned the barrels tighter. Then there were a couple more pretty good runs but I noticed the horses were having more trouble on the turns. The dirt around the barrels was getting so churned up that the horses were slipping on it. Raine must be one of the last riders. I wished she'd go. I was getting nervous. Another horse had trouble on the third barrel, seemed to slide a little, and wound up knocking over the barrel.

Then I saw Raine and Fox out in the alleyway, ready

to make a running entrance into the arena. Fox was dancing and tossing her head, but Raine had her under control. Suddenly she loosened the reins and leaned forward. Fox shot into the arena like she was nuclear powered. The first barrel, clean as a whistle. Down to the second one. Around the figure eight, Fox's powerfully muscled hindquarters driving her around the turn. The long run to the third barrel. The crowd was screaming. This had to be at least as fast as the palomino —and Raine was their hometown girl! I was yelling my head off.

Around the last barrel. All right! She was going to run clean. No barrels down. She was turning for home — when Fox's hind legs, driving hard for speed, hit that patch of loose dirt. I saw her start to slide and tip. At the speed and angle she was moving it looked more like a motorcycle wreck than a horse falling. With Raine still in the saddle, Fox hit the ground sideways and slid to a stop in a cloud of dust. The cheers of the crowd turned into an ominous groan and for a second all I could see was Fox's scrambling hoofs and Raine's blue shirt all mixed up together out there in the dust.

I don't remember running but the next thing I knew I was out there beside Raine. Steve was there too, reaching out to grab the dangling reins as Fox lunged to her feet, wild-eyed and snorting.

I was on my knees beside Raine. Dimly, I noticed that there were people all over the place, crowding in and giving each other all kinds of orders, but all I could see was Raine. Why was she lying there so still with her eyes closed? A headline flashed across my mind. LOCAL GIRL DIES IN FREAK RODEO ACCIDENT.

"Raine!" I guess I was yelling at the top of my voice. There was no answer. Panicking, I looked up, straight into my brother's face. It was dead white and there was a kind of desperation in his eyes. For the first time I could remember, I was seeing Steve scared — just as scared as I was.

A small sound jerked my attention back to Raine. She turned her head and moaned softly. I reached for her hand. "Raine," I said, my voice going shaky with relief. "It's gonna be okay. The ambulance is coming. Just don't move, okay?"

Suddenly, her eyes popped wide open. "Ambulance!" she echoed, her voice very loud for a dying person. "I don't need an ambulance. And for cryin' out loud let go of my hand. Everybody's looking at us." The next thing I knew she was sitting up. "What happened any . . ." Her face went stiff with terror. "Fox!"

"She's okay," Steve cut in, in his old calm, almost-bored tone. "You and her ain't settin' any barrel-racing records but you both sure know how to take a fall."

Instantly the fear was gone from Raine's face. "Shut up, Steve!" she snarled, scrambling to her feet and jerking the reins out of his hand.

"Whoa now, young lady," old Jake Williams, the arena director, said. "Maybe you should just stay put until the doctor comes and makes sure nothin's broke."

Raine gave him a blistering glare. "Don't 'young lady' me, Jake. I'm just fine and I'm gettin' out of here *now*."

She grabbed her slightly squashed hat that some cowboy was holding out to her gallantly, gave Fox's reins a pull, and limping slightly, set off across the arena, scattering the crowd that had gathered around. Steve and I fell in beside her. There was a cheer from the crowd as we passed the grandstand but Raine, red-faced and embarrassed, kept her eyes on the ground ahead of her.

Thirteen

*A*ll the way to where we'd parked the truck, Raine didn't say a word. She look mad enough to swallow lead and spit bullets. I moved up beside her. "Hey," I said, "don't take it so hard. It wasn't your fault. Anybody could have slipped the way that dirt was worked up."

She shot me a glance. "Yeah? Well it didn't happen to *anybody*. It happened to me. Fox was making the best run of her life and I had to turn her too sharp and put her right into that soft spot."

We were at the trailer now. Raine took off Fox's bridle, put the halter on, and tied her to the side of the trailer. Then she walked around the horse, running her hands down each leg, double checking for any sign of an injury, muttering apologies to Fox and insults to herself all the way around.

"Will you quit blaming yourself?" I said.

Before she could answer, Steve cut in. "Leave her alone, Beau. The rich girl's pride got a little bruised. She'll heal."

Raine swung around to face him, her eyes giving off grey sparks.

"Hey, Raine, tough luck," a friendly voice behind us interrupted just in time to save my brother from serious injury. It was Darcy Sanderson and a couple of other guys we knew who rodeoed a little. If they noticed the conversation around here was a little tense they didn't let on, and in a few minutes things had relaxed considerably.

Of course I had to introduce Steve to them and I could see the wheels going around in their heads as they studied him, trying to figure out how this punk in the leather jacket and T-shirt fit in with me. Good luck, guys, I thought. When you get the answer, let me know.

It would be a couple of hours till I rode, so we all decided to go watch some of the other events. The calf roping was on when we got back to the arena. Not exactly my idea of a real exciting contest — a hundred-and-fifty-pound man and a thousand-pound horse against a two-hundred-pound calf.

I was sitting there trying to pick out familiar faces in the grandstand across the arena when Raine dug me in the ribs with her elbow. "Guess who," she said, her voice full of cold contempt. I followed the direction of her gaze and focused in on the next roper just maneuvering his big grey horse into position behind the barrier. That horse looked familiar. And so did the big, heavy-set rider . . .

"Good old Russ Donovan," I said.

Raine nodded. "I was hoping he'd left the country."

I glanced over at Steve. His face was cool and expressionless, giving nothing away, but he was watching Donovan and I would have given a lot to know what he was thinking. He and Donovan had a score to settle — and I doubted that either one had forgotten.

Then Donovan's calf was streaking across the arena with the big grey horse right behind, perfectly positioned for the throw of the loop.

The rope sailed out, a good straight throw. The calf ran into the loop — but Donovan had made one of those split-second miscalculations that cost cowboys a lot of money. He was too slow gathering slack. Even as the grey sat down on his haunches and slid to a dusty stop, it was too late. Donovan was already piling out of the saddle before he realized what had happened. The calf had run right through the loop. He stood there for a couple of seconds staring after the calf that was hightailing it for the far end of the arena as the crowd laughed and groaned all at once.

Then he spun on his heel and strode back toward the horse, which was stepping backward, trying its best to do its job of tightening the rope after the calf is caught. Donovan reached out and grabbed the reins, yanking the horse to a stop. The horse threw up its head as the bit jerked its mouth, side-stepped nervously, and then stood still as Donovan mounted. He pulled its head around and galloped out of the arena.

"Ol' Donovan sure don't like to lose," Darcy said with a grin.

"Knowing him, he's probably got himself convinced it was the horse's fault," I said.

"Donovan's a born loser," Raine said.

That seemed to pretty well cover the subject of Donovan. Nobody mentioned him again as we sat talking and half-heartedly watching the roping for another few minutes.

I was starting to get restless. "I'm going down to the bucking chutes," I said, standing up.

Automatically Raine stood up too — and Steve. "It'll

be quite a while yet till I ride,'' I told him. "Go ahead and watch the roping if you want.''

Steve shrugged and grinned lazily. "I'll pass,'' he said. "When you've seen one calf roper you've seen 'em all. Besides, I don't want to miss out on any of your technique. I might learn something.''

I glared at him. I didn't need any of his razzing in front of all these other guys.

For a minute there, I was afraid they were *all* going to trail on down to watch me get ready for this great ride, but fortunately, Sanderson's appetite got the better of him and he decided he had to head to the concession for a hamburger and the other guys tagged along.

The three of us walked on down past the holding corrals where the horses were. I'd drawn a horse I'd never heard of. His name was The Saint and I thought I'd check to see if any of the broncs happened to be wearing a halo.

"There he is,'' Raine announced, pointing to the ugliest-looking Roman-nosed pinto I'd ever dreamed of meeting. "That's gotta be him. The Saint is definitely a pinto name.''

I never got a chance to explore that logic, because right then, a scream ripped through the hot afternoon.

In spite of the heat, that sound sent a cold wave of goose pimples marching up my spine. "What is that?'' Raine asked, her voice almost a whisper. But there wasn't time for an answer because the scream came again — from somewhere behind the announcer's stand. All three of us started to run.

It wasn't until the third scream that I realized the sound wasn't coming from a human. It was a horse. One that was either hurt bad or scared out of its mind. Or maybe both.

Then we came around the corner and I suddenly

understood. What I saw just about made me sick — but it didn't surprise me any. It was Russ Donovan. He had his grey gelding backed into the corner of a holding pen, working him over with a heavy braided quirt.

Keeping a short grip on the reins with his left hand, he swung the whip with his right. The lash whined viciously through the air and hit the gray's shoulder with a sickening crack. The horse squealed, reared, and fought to get away, but Donovan controlled it with a violent jerk of the reins.

Raine got to the corral a couple of steps ahead of me. "Stop it, Donovan!" she burst out, her voice shaking with anger. She started to unlatch the corral gate, but instinctively I grabbed her arm. Crossing Donovan when he was in a mood like this was dangerous.

"No, Raine, stay . . . " I began, but the sentence never got finished. Because right then, Steve went over the fence. He jumped down from the top rail and landed like a cat behind Donovan.

Donovan was so busy beating the horse he didn't even notice. "You lazy, gutless . . . " he rasped between breaths as he raised the whip again.

"That's enough, Donovan." Steve's voice was low but it cut just like the whip. Donovan's arm froze in mid-air. He lowered the whip. His left hand released its grip on the reins and the horse plunged away to stand trembling in the far corner of the corral. Then, white with rage, Donovan turned to face Steve.

"*You* again!" he snarled. "You cocky little know-it-all city punk. You ditched my truck, then you moved in and took over my job, and now you think you're gonna tell me how to handle my horse. Well, you can think again, you . . . " His voice grated like steel on stone as he went on to call my brother every name I'd ever heard and even a few I hadn't.

Steve just looked at him, his face expressionless, totally cool, and — at least as far as it showed on the outside — unafraid. I looked at the two of them standing there facing each other. Donovan was probably thirty years old, over six feet tall, and at least two hundred pounds of muscle and meanness, up against a nineteen-year-old kid, four inches shorter, fifty pounds lighter, and a whole lot stupider, just for being there.

But then, I shouldn't have been surprised. Steve spent more time fighting in school that he ever did learning. I can still remember Pop shaking his head as he plastered Steve in bandages for about the third time in one week. ''I know it's hopeless to tell you to quit fighting,'' he'd said wearily, ''but I just wish that for once in your life you'd pick on a little guy.''

I glanced at the crowd that had gathered. I knew a lot of them. They were cowboys mostly, people who respected their animals, and I doubted there was a single one of them who could stomach the way Donovan had been abusing that horse. But it was Steve who had made the first move. Steve who never thought about the consequences. And now it was his fight . . .

Donovan had finally run out of breath and vocabulary and now he stood glaring at Steve with rattlesnake eyes, daring him to make the first move.

Steve gave him a cool, mocking half-smile. ''You know a lot of words, don't you, Donovan?'' he said, his voice soft but taunting. ''And you're a real tough dude when it comes to beatin' up animals that can't fight back. Wonder what you'd do against somebody who *did* fight back.''

Donovan's face registered something close to disbelief. It must have been a long time since anybody had dared challenge him. A poisonous smile crept across his lips.

"Okay, bleeding heart," he hissed, "you got it. I won't hurt the poor little horse. You need this worse than he does anyhow."

Even before the words were out, I knew what was going to happen. "Look out, Steve!" I yelled, as I saw the muscles in Donovan's shoulder start to flex. But it was too late. Donovan swung the whip in a sizzling arc and it caught Steve full in the face, half blinding him. He staggered backward, wiping his hand across his eyes and smearing the thin line of blood that had magically appeared from the corner of his left eyebrow and along his cheekbone to the hairline.

Donovan swung the whip again, catching Steve across the throat this time. Coughing, Steve went down on his knees. Instantly, he was up again, staggering a little, still trying to get his breath. But Donovan didn't let up. He swung the whip again and again, never letting Steve within reach. Steve tried to dodge sideways but his boots slipped on the trampled grass. He fell and Donovan moved in, towering over him, cracking the whip like a lion tamer at the circus.

Raine's hand tightened on my arm. "He's gonna kill him, Beau," she whispered in a choked voice, and I was afraid she was right.

Furiously, I looked around at the crowd. Somebody must be going to stop this thing. But it was like they were all at a circus too, watching but not a part of what they were seeing. Well, maybe a dozen or more big, tough cowboys could stand and watch Steve get beaten to death but I couldn't. He was my brother . . .

I broke loose from Raine's grip and started to tear open the gate latch, but suddenly a strong hand on my shoulder jerked me back. I spun around and found myself looking into a big, dark, familiar face. It belonged to Harry Screaming Eagle, one of the best ropers and bulldoggers in the country — and a one-time partner of Donovan's.

"Stay out of it, Beau," he warned quietly. "Your brother started it. Let him finish it. It's not over yet."

I jerked free of Harry's hand and gave him a defiant look. "Yeah," I muttered bitterly, "it ain't over. Steve's still breathin'."

But I knew better than to try again. Harry had spelled it out and that's how things were. Steve was the outsider, the city punk who'd come onto cowboy turf, made an enemy of a cowboy, taken his job, and then challenged him to fight. I knew there wasn't a whole lot of love lost on Russ Donovan around here and I would have bet that if Steve hadn't jumped in to stop him from beating the horse, somebody else would have. But Steve had done it. And around here, when you start something it's up to you to finish it.

Harry was right. It wasn't over yet. Steve was hurt, he was outclassed in weight and strength, and he didn't have a chance. Everybody knew it — but no one had remembered to tell him. He was on his feet again and staggering *toward* Donovan.

Back off, Steve! Quit while you still can! I wanted to scream, but all of a sudden, something happened. It was so fast I'm still not sure what I saw. Donovan had raised the whip again, I know that. Then, the next thing I knew, Steve's foot slashed through the air and his hard-soled riding boot connected with Donovan's hand with a sound like a horse's hoof slamming against flesh. The whip went spinning out of Donovan's numbed hand. In one lightning move, Steve bent down and grabbed it and sent it flying over the fence. A roar of approval went up from the crowd. All of a sudden this was turning into something like a fair fight.

For a second Donovan stood stunned, rubbing his wrist. That was enough for Steve. All the fury that had built up in him exploded and he was all over Donovan with both fists. He must have got in five or six good punches before Donovan knew what hit him and for one crazy second I really believed that Steve was going to pound him into the ground.

I should have known better. Donovan was a street fighter from way back and he could take the same kind of punishment he handed out. He shook his head and came back with a vicious jab to the ribs that bent Steve over and left him wide open for a right to the jaw that almost decked him. Dazed, Steve let his guard down and that gave Donovan the chance he was waiting for. With a roar like a wounded bear, he grabbed Steve around the waist, and with the strength that made throwing two-hundred-pound calves look easy, lifted him off his feet and threw him down. Steve hit the ground with a force that should have broken his back. It knocked the wind out of him and he lay there gasping for air as Donovan moved in for the kill. Donovan hesitated, looking down at Steve as he started to struggle weakly to his knees. Don't get up Steve, I begged silently. You got in some good shots but you know you're beat. Don't get up and he'll leave you alone.

That's what I *thought*. I was wrong. Slowly, Donovan wiped his hand across his nose, which was bleeding pretty good from one Steve's punches. He stared at the blood in disbelief — as if he hadn't known it was possible for anyone to make him bleed. His face warped into a mask of fury, and without warning, he kicked Steve in the ribs with all his strength. With a half-smothered groan, Steve crumpled into a heap on the ground.

This time Donovan had gone too far. There was an

angry roar from the crowd and half a dozen guys started to move forward. One of them was me.

But Donovan was already bringing his boot back for another kick. Unbelievably, this time he missed. Because Steve wasn't there. He was rolling out of the way, and in the same movement, reaching out to grab Donovan's foot before he could get his balance back. Donovan hit the ground like a giant spruce that's been snapped in a windstorm.

And then Steve was on him. I'd never seen anybody fight the way he did. I know it wasn't just plain old down-and-dirty street fighting. He wasn't just using punches. It was some kind of a combination of chops and kicks and fists that looked like The Karate Kid had somehow got crossed with The Terminator and the whole thing had gone out of control.

One thing for sure, it didn't seem to matter how big your opponent was. He fell just as hard. And Donovan fell. He must have got up about three times, but every time, Steve decked him again. The fourth time, he stayed down.

Steve was on his feet — barely. He stood over Donovan, swaying a little. The sound of his ragged breathing was loud in the sudden silence that fell over the crowd. "Come on, Donovan," he panted hoarsely, "get up and fight." Under all the dirt and blood, Steve's face was dead white, but it was set with the same determination I could remember from when he was a little kid. Looking at the two of them, I would have bet that Steve was in a lot worse shape than Donovan was, but Steve was the one on his feet. Because he wanted to be.

I felt a movement beside me and saw Harry Screaming Eagle easing his way past me and into the corral. He moved up beside Steve kind of careful, the way you'd go up to a dog you thought might bite. "All right, kid,"

Harry said quietly. "Settle down. You beat him. It's over."

Steve shook his head. "No it ain't," he said. "Not quite." Then, holding his side, he walked slowly over to where the grey was standing, still white-eyed and shivering. "Easy boy," he said softly, reaching out to lay his hand on the horse's sweaty face. He gathered up the reins and then uncinched the saddle. Teeth clenched against the pain in his side, he dragged the saddle off and dropped it on the ground. Then he found a baler twine hanging on the fence, looped it around the horse's neck, and slipped off the bridle. He dropped it on top of the saddle, and half leaning on the horse for support, he led it over to where Donovan was just beginning to moan and twitch a little.

Nobody in the crowd moved. They all just stood there, silent, wondering what was coming next as Steve reached into his jeans pocket. His hand came out with a roll of bills. One at time, he dropped them in the dirt beside Donovan. Mentally, I counted as they fell. One hundred, two hundred, three hundred, four, five, five-fifty, six, six-twenty, six-forty, six-forty-five — two loonies caught the light as they cartwheeled down to land with a metallic thud.

"Six hundred and forty-seven dollars," Steve said, still breathing hard. "That's all I've got and considering the shape he's in, it should be enough. I just bought this horse."

He started to lead the grey toward the gate and I opened it for him, but suddenly, Harry Screaming Eagle's deep voice cut the stillness. "No," he said. Steve turned to face him, and I caught the flash of anger in my brother's eyes. I knew then that, even beat up so bad he could hardly stand, Steve would fight Harry too, if that's what it took to walk out of there with the horse.

But Harry didn't say another word. He just pulled a pack of cigarettes from his pocket, tore the back off, and wrote something on it. Then he handed it to the cowboy standing closest to him. He read it, grinned, wrote something too, and passed it on. The piece of cardboard circulated through the whole crowd. Finally, it came back to Harry. He leaned over Donovan, fastened a big hand on his shirt collar, and dragged him into a half-sitting position. Then he jammed the pen in Donovan's hand and held the cardboard against his knee. "Sign it," he said.

Donovan stared, rubbed a hand across his battered face, and finally caught on. "What the . . . " he began, but Harry cut him off.

"Sign it or I'll turn the kid loose on you again." Donovan glared at Harry through the eye that wasn't swelling shut. Then he looked at Steve. I did, too — and wondered how anybody who had to lean against a horse to keep from falling over could still look so dangerous.

Donovan swore and glared around the circle of cowboys like he expected someone to speak up for him. Nobody did. He scrawled something on the cardboard and shoved it back at Harry.

I stepped closer and read:

Sold to Steve Garrett — one grey gelding
PAID IN FULL

Underneath was Donovan's scrawled signature and below that there were at least fifteen signatures.

It had to be the weirdest horse deal in Alberta history, but it sure looked legal to me.

Harry nodded with satisfaction and handed the cardboard to Steve. "Okay, Garrett," he said, "take your horse and get out of here.'' Then his voice softened and something close to a smile came across his weathered face. ''Nobody can say you didn't earn him!''

Steve nodded. His eyes locked on Harry's for a second and something I figured might have been respect passed between them. Then Steve turned and led the horse away. Raine and I fell into step on either side of him.

I looked back once and saw that Donovan was on his feet. His eyes met mine with a look so evil I turned away. Steve had won the fight but from now on he'd have to watch his back.

Fourteen

I breathed a sigh of relief when we were around the corner and out of sight of the crowd. It felt like the first breath I'd taken in a long time.

Then I turned to see how Steve was doing. He was looking pretty rough by now. I figured he'd been running on pure adrenaline but even that was about to run out. "Hey," I said, "why don't you just wait here a minute. I'll go bring the truck over." He ignored me and kept walking.

We were almost to the trailer when he handed me the end of the twine he was leading the horse with. "Go ahead and load him" he said tiredly, "but be careful with him. He's had a rough day."

Steve was right about that. I figured that after being beat up and scared half to death the grey was going to be tough to load. But I was wrong. Even with just the baler twine around his neck, he walked right up into the trailer. When Fox laid her ears back and gave him a threatening look from the far side of the partition, he just edged over a little farther to his side and stood there minding his own business. He had to be about the best-natured horse I'd ever seen — which made me so mad at Russ Donovan I would have liked to go back and hit him a couple of times myself.

But right now I figured we'd better get Steve home. He was leaning against the side of the trailer with his eyes closed, looking like he was about to pass out any minute. I closed up the trailer and opened the door on the passenger side of the truck. "Come on," I said, "Get in before you fall down."

He opened his eyes — and shook his head. "Can't go yet," he said.

"Why not?" I asked, wondering if he had a rematch planned.

"You got a bronc to ride."

Before I could answer that, Raine cut in and said something downright rude about the bronc riding. Steve *really* opened his eyes then, stared at her, and started to laugh. That was a mistake. The laugh, I mean. Suddenly he winced and doubled over holding his side, and the laugh downgraded into a groan. He took a couple of deep breaths and then glared up at Raine. "Make me laugh again and I'll break your neck," he muttered from between clenched teeth. Then he looked at me. "Sure you don't want to ride, Beau? I can wait."

"No you can't," I said. "Get in the truck."

He shrugged — and for the first time in living memory, did what he was told.

"Catch, Beau," Raine said. I looked up — and just managed to catch the truck keys in my hand instead of my eye. Raine climbed in beside Steve and we headed for home.

The road between the rodeo grounds and home seemed to have got a lot longer and a lot rougher in the last couple of hours. I tried to miss the potholes but I couldn't miss them all. By the time we hit the edge of town I figured Steve was either unconscious or wishing he was. His eyes were closed and his head was half on Raine's shoulder. She had her arm around him, trying to hold him steady against the jolting of the truck.

"How you doin', Steve?" I asked.

He didn't answer but Raine gave me a worried look. "He's really hurt, Beau," she said softly.

I nodded. "We're almost there." I down-shifted and signalled to turn onto Fenton's first side street.

Right then Steve opened his eyes. "Where do you think you're goin'?" he asked. He tried to sit up straight, winced, and changed his mind.

"Just don't try to move. We'll have you at the hospital in a minute."

This time he did sit up straight. "Oh, no, you won't."

"Don't be stupid, Steve." Raine said. "You've at least gotta let them check and see if anything's broken."

Steve shifted position enough to give Raine a long, level look. "I don't 'gotta' do nothin'," he said.

The look on Raine's face just then was interesting. For probably the first time in her life she couldn't seem to think of anything to say.

I gave it a try. "Look, Steve," I began, as I started to wheel the truck into the hospital parking lot. That was as far as I got — at either wheeling or talking.

Steve's bloody-knuckled left hand clamped down on my wrist like a vice. "Beau," he said quietly. "There's two things I don't mess with. One's doctors and the other's cops. You drag me into that hospital and I'm gonna end up mixed up with both."

The truck eased to a stop in the middle of the road while I sat there thinking about what he'd said — and about what he *hadn't* said. He was probably right about the cops getting into the picture once the hospital people had a look at him and found out he got this way in a fight. Maybe we could say he'd had an accident — been trampled by a horse or something. Sure, Beau, great idea. And the horse hit him half a dozen times with a whip? Try again.

But mostly what I kept thinking about was that night coming back from Calgary when he outran the cops. All along I'd been trying to tell myself that he'd just been showing off, that it was just that crazy stubborn streak of his that made him risk killing us all to avoid a forty-dollar ticket. I'd been having a little trouble believing myself all along. Now I knew I was lying. I also knew I had a choice to make, fast. Steve couldn't stop me if I decided to drive up to that emergency entrance right now . . .

I was blocking traffic. The guy behind me was leaning on his horn. Steve let go of my arm. Our eyes met. I turned off the signal light. "Okay," I said wearily. "Let's go home."

Steve managed a crooked grin and closed his eyes. Raine and I exchanged glances. Neither of us said anything.

Five minutes later we were pulling up beside our house. Steve half opened his eyes. "You gonna take care of my horse, Beau?" he asked in kind of a faraway voice.

"Sure," I said, "Just as soon as we get you into the house."

"I can get into the house by myself," he said, easing himself out the passenger door behind Raine.

"Sure you can, Steve," Raine said, calmly reaching out to catch him just as his knees started to buckle.

I grabbed him from the other side and we half dragged him into the house and laid him half-conscious on the couch.

"Go ahead and unload the horse," Raine said, helping herself to the only two clean towels left on the bathroom shelf. "I'll try and clean him up a little."

"I can wash my own face," Steve said, easing himself up to a sitting position.

Raine tossed her hair back. "If you're feeling good enough to sit up, you can sit up here by the table where I can see what I'm doing."

"Not likely, lady," Steve said.

I put the grey in the little barn that was attached to Pop's shop, fed and watered him, and then checked him for injuries. He had four or five welts across his shoulder and flank where Donovan had hit him, and in one place the skin was broken, but there was nothing seriously wrong with him that a little decent handling wouldn't cure. I left him happily munching hay and headed back to the house.

I stopped at the kitchen doorway. Steve was sitting by the table — right where Raine had put him — sitting astride the chair and smoking a cigarette. I noticed that he had changed his filthy jeans — into a pair that were clean but missing both knees. He really did need to buy some clothes, I thought, especially since those were *my* holey jeans he had on. His ripped T-shirt — *another* Billy Idol — was lying with his jeans on top of the garbage can. Variety wasn't a big feature of Steve's wardrobe.

Raine had a pot of steaming water and a big bottle of antiseptic set out on the table and she was busy dabbing at his face with a wet towel. I hesitated in the doorway for a minute, taking in the scene. I'd never really figured Raine was cut out to be a nurse.

I may have been right about that, because right then

Steve bellowed, "Ouch! Are you tryin' to blind me or what? Stop drippin' that iodine in my eye."

"It's not iodine, it's Dettol. Now stop being such a baby and sit still."

I swallowed a grin and walked in to see how bad Donovan had rearranged Steve's face. Actually, with the dirt and blood washed off he looked even worse. He had a cut lip and a swollen purple bruise on one cheekbone, but what sent a shiver up my spine was the thin red line that Donovan's quirt had left across my brother's face, and into his eyebrow. A quarter-inch lower and Steve would have lost an eye . . .

"Steve," I said, "can you see out of that eye okay?"

"Yeah, amazingly enough after Florence Nightingale here got done trying' to wash it out with battery acid."

His hands were in worse shape than his face, the knuckles skinned and raw, but I figured Steve didn't mind that — considering it was Donovan's face he'd skinned them on.

There were a couple of raw welts across his arms and shoulders where the whip had caught him but that was just surface stuff. The only thing that looked really bad was his side, where Donovan's boot had left a big, swollen, purple-green bruise. I could tell by the way Steve was sitting that it was hurting pretty good already and I figured it was going to get worse before it got better.

Raine must have come to the same conclusion. "You've got some broken ribs, you know," she said.

Steve looked at her. "No kiddin'."

"Well, you can't just ignore them and hope they'll go away. You need a doctor or at least we've got to bandage them up or . . . "

"Raine," Steve interrupted, "do me a favor."

Raine eyed him suspiciously. "What?"

"Go home."

Raine took a step back and stared at him. "What?"

"You heard me. I've had all the medical care I can handle in one day and I ain't about to do chores this afternoon, so you and Beau better get started early."

Raine looked at me. I shrugged. "Yeah, I guess it's gonna take a while to get all the stuff done that we rushed through this morning." I turned to Steve. "You sure you'll be okay here by yourself?"

Steve gave me his old arrogant grin — which came out a little crooked with his cut lip. "No, Beauregard, I ain't sure. Actually, what I've got planned is to die the minute you get out the door so you'll have this big, untidy body underfoot when you get home. Any more stupid questions before you go?"

I sighed and gave up. "No sense, no feeling," I said wearily. "Let's go, Raine."

Looking like a storm about to cut loose, Raine tossed the towel over the back of a chair, dumped the water down the sink, and without a look in Steve's direction, headed for the door.

She was halfway out when Steve stopped her. "Raine."

She flung a smouldering look in his direction. He grinned at her. "Thanks," he said.

The door shut, hard.

Steve gave me an innocent look. "She mad or something?"

Fifteen

Raine and I drove over to the Quarter Circle in total silence. She pulled the truck up in front of the barn and then just sat there for a minute. I figured she had something to say, so I sat and waited. Finally she turned to face me. "Beau," she said in kind of a hushed voice, "do you think he killed somebody?"

"What?"

"Don't play games with me, Beau. You know exactly what I mean and you must have asked yourself the same thing a few dozen times by now."

I sighed, leaned my head back against the seat, and closed my eyes. This day must have gone on for about ten years already and I didn't have the energy to get into this heavy-duty conversation. "I don't want to talk about it right now, Raine."

"Yeah, and you never will, Beau, 'cause when it comes to hiding your head in the sand you've got more talent than the average ostrich. But we are going to talk about it. You and I both know that Steve is running from something and I think it's about time we found out what."

"You could try asking him," I said.

She gave me a scornful look. "Yeah, and I could try out for Miss Universe too."

"So what do you expect me to do? Call the cops and turn my own brother in because he *acts* like he *might* have done something?"

Raine turned kind of red and her usually steady gaze wavered a little. "No," she said in a small voice, "but . . . "

"Anyway," I said, "whatever Steve is, he's not a killer."

Raine's eyes came up to meet mine again. "How do you know?"

"That knife he carries. He had it with him today and he could have used it on Donovan and claimed self-defence. But he didn't. Donovan used every dirty trick in the book to half kill him but Steve fought fair. He's always fought fair."

"Maybe," Raine said, "but I still think he's dangerous."

I couldn't argue with that. I *knew* he was dangerous. And yet, after what I'd seen today, there was something in that kind of dangerous that I couldn't help but admire. "Look, Raine," I said, "if you don't want him around any more, just say so. Tell your mom it ain't workin' out and forget the whole thing. You don't owe Steve anything."

She sighed and shook her head. "No, I can't do that," she said slowly. "I know what you're thinking, Beau. But it's not just because we'll lose the horses if we lose Steve." She paused and then added, "Sure, that's part of it. At first, that was all of it. But now, I don't know,

Beau. I think he needs to be here as bad as we need him here, and . . . Is any of this making sense, Beau?''

I nodded. ''Yeah, a whole lot of sense.''

She went on. ''And what he did today. It was right. He's got more guts than anybody I ever met.''

''And less brains.''

She laughed but then her face turned serious again. ''And what he's been doing around here, with the horses, and all the other work. It's great. He's worth ten Russ Donovans.''

''I think Donovan found that out today.''

''No kiddin','' Raine said, smiling a little, ''and it couldn't have happened to a nicer guy. But Steve still scares me.''

I thought about that for a minute, not really understanding. From the first time she'd laid eyes on Steve she had stood up to him. Most of the time *she* had been the one to pick the fights. Now, all of a sudden, he scared her?

''Hey,'' I said, ''that tough act he puts on around you isn't for real, you know. He'd never do anything to hurt you.''

For a minute Raine sat there silent, absent-mindedly dusting the radio knobs with her finger. Then her eyes met mine. ''I know,'' she said. ''Maybe that's what scares me.''

Suddenly she opened the door and headed for the corral. The only thing we talked about for the next couple of hours was horses.

It was on into the evening when we finished the chores and Raine dropped me off at home. There weren't any lights on in the house.

I opened the door. ''Steve?''

There was no answer. I turned on the lights and walked on into the living room. Steve was lying on the couch, tossing restlessly in his sleep. His face was wet with sweat. It was hot in the house but I didn't figure it was *that* hot. He looked pretty sick to me. I shut off the lights to keep from waking him and went around opening windows to try and cool him off. He kept tossing around and muttering something. At first I thought he was talking to me. Then I realized I was wrong.

I leaned over to catch the words. " . . . You're gonna pay, Romero. You killed her. I'm gonna make you pay real good."

A sudden cold wave swept through my insides. I remembered the words I'd said to Raine just a couple of hours ago. And I wondered if I believed them any more . . .

Steve muttered something I couldn't understand, swore, and then, "I got you, Romero. You'll never get another chance to . . . "

Suddenly I didn't want to hear any more. If Steve wanted to tell me something, I'd listen, but this wasn't the way to hear it.

I reached out and shook his shoulder. "Steve? Hey, come on, man, wake up. You're having nightmares or somethin'."

He sighed and then all of a sudden he was sitting up, his eyes wide open and wild. He was breathing hard. "Where is she? Where'd they take her?" He started to get up, groaned, and fell back on the couch. "I've gotta find . . . "

Recognition edged back into his eyes. "Beau?" he whispered.

"Yeah, it's me," I said softly, kneeling beside him, trying to calm him down the only way I knew, the way I treat a panicked colt caught in a barbed-wire fence.

"Easy, Steve. Just take it easy. It's all over now." I didn't know what *it* was, and I sure as heck didn't know if it was over, but it sounded like the right thing to say at the time.

Slowly, Steve's breathing slowed down. His eyes were still shadowed with a pain that wasn't all physical, but that glazed wildness was gone. "Beau, what . . . ?" he began, his voice not much more than a whisper.

"It's okay," I said reassuringly. "You were just delirious or having a nightmare or somethin'."

His eyes locked on mine. "What did I say?"

I saw the fear in my brother's eyes, and I knew I couldn't tell him the truth. He didn't need any more on his mind tonight.

I shrugged. "Nothing I could understand. Mostly you were just moaning and groaning and tossing around." His eyes searched my face for a few long seconds, but I kept my gaze level and steady.

At last he sighed and relaxed. "Thanks, Beau," he said.

"You better get some more sleep. You look like hell warmed over."

Steve managed a weak grin. "Yeah? Well that's nothin' compared to what I feel like. It's too hot in here to sleep anyhow," he said. He eased himself off the couch to go stand in the open door and stare into the silent darkness outside.

"Anything I can get you?" I asked awkwardly. I'm not real good at looking after people.

"Got any cold water in this place?"

"Sure. I'll get you some."

I stood by the bathroom sink, waiting for the water to run ice cold — and trying not to think about what Steve had said in his sleep. It didn't *have* to mean anything. Maybe he was sick enough to be raving out of his head. I knew Donovan had hurt him a lot worse than he was letting on. The amount of pain he was in, he was going to have a pretty rough night, I thought, staring absent-mindedly at my reflection in the mirror on the medicine cabinet. And that's when I got an idea.

"Here," I said, handing Steve a glass of water. I also handed him a little drugstore bottle with four big orange capsules rattling around in it. "Try a couple of these. They're some kind of high-voltage pain killers. The doctor gave 'em to Pop last time his knee went out. He only used a few of them so I snuck a couple last spring when I sprained my ankle playing football. I don't know what's in 'em but it sure works. Man, I felt so good I could've gone back out and played football. I almost finished the bottle in the next couple of days before Pop caught me and made me go back to aspirins."

Steve gave me a strange look as he slowly reached out for the bottle. His eyes swept over it and came back to me again. The muscles in his forearm flexed as his hand tightened on the bottle. "I never thought you were this stupid, Beau," he said in a voice gone as cold as his eyes. Suddenly he spun around and threw the pill bottle out into the darkness. It hit the porch railing and bounced off the bottom step. In the glow of the porch light, orange pills ricocheted like escapees from a pinball machine. Then, with a sound like a half-smothered sob, he picked up the glass of water and threw it too. It exploded like a rifle shot in the stillness. Pieces of glass fell to the ground with little tinkling sounds.

Then, nothing. Just a sudden dead silence in the night, broken only by our breathing. I stood there staring at Steve. I was thinking about what Raine had said — about him being dangerous, I mean.

He just stood there, silhouetted by the porch light, staring into space and breathing like he'd run a long way.

He turned to look at me. I don't know what he read on my face. Fear, maybe. He ran his hand through his hair and shook his head. "Look, Beau," he began uncertainly, "I didn't mean . . . " He stopped, tried again. "You don't understand . . . ."

I looked him right in the eye. Anger was beginning to replace shock in my mind. "You're right, Steve," I said. "I don't understand. So why don't you try explaining things so I _do_."

Our eyes locked and there was a long silence. He swallowed, took a deep breath, and for a minute there I really thought he was going to break down and trust me. I should have known better. He turned away and shook his head. "I'm sorry, Beau," he said, his voice soft and rough at the same time. "I can't." At the instant, I knew instinctively that if he hadn't been busted up so bad he'd have been gone right then. Instead, he walked stiffly over to one of the old lawn chairs that sit on the porch and sank down into it. "Go on in and get some sleep, Beau," he said. "I'm gonna stay out here."

For a minute, I hesitated. Then the next thing I knew I was hauling the other chair over beside Steve and sitting down. Don't ask me why. I was dog-tired and spending a sleepless night beside this psycho guy wasn't going to help any. But I knew I couldn't leave him there alone. Whoever he was, he was still my brother.

We sat there in the darkness for a long time, listening to the night sounds. An owl was hooting lonesomely somewhere to the west, little critters rustled in the tall grass along the lane once in a while. Against the starlit sky I could see Willie/Billy sitting on top of a fence post, waiting for one of those rustles to come within pouncing range.

I could hear Steve's breathing. It was uneven, like it

hurt. "You asleep?" I whispered. I knew it was a stupid question but I hadn't had much luck with my intelligent questions so far.

"No. Why, are you?"

I ignored that. "How you feelin'?"

"Guess," he said, shifting position with a muffled groan. "We got any ice?"

"I dunno. If I go find some what are you gonna throw it at?" Okay, so maybe it was a cheap shot but I was still pretty burnt about my last attempt at playing doctor. There was a long silence. I could feel Steve looking at me and was glad it was too dark to have to look back. I stood up and stretched. "Okay, okay, I'm going."

I spent some time digging around in the top of the fridge. Pop and I aren't exactly in the habit of regular defrosting. In the very back I came upon the container of tiger ice cream Pop had bought for my fifteenth birthday. I looked inside and found three tablespoons of ice-crystalled ice cream which I ate right then and there. I'd missed supper, and besides, that was one less thing to fit back in the freezing compartment.

About the only thing I didn't find in there was ice — so I settled for the next best thing.

"Here," I said to Steve, handing him a flat, brown-paper package.

He took it. "What in . . . " he began, holding the package up to catch the dim glow of the porch light. "Beau," he said disgustedly, "I sent you for ice to put on my ribs and you come back with a T-bone? I ain't hungry, I'm hurtin'."

"I know. But there ain't any ice. Be resourceful. I cured a black eye with a chuck steak last year after Tom Willis called me 'beautiful' for the third time and we had a little discussion about it. At least I got you a *good* steak. Put it on your ribs overnight and it'll be thawed out in time for breakfast.''

Steve groaned — and muttered something I chose not to hear. But he settled back in the chair, holding the steak against his side.

''How's it feel?''

''Like a chunk of dead cow. How'd you expect it to feel?''

I slouched down in my chair, trying to get comfortable and wishing I wasn't going to be awake all night.

The next thing I knew, the early-morning sun was shining in my face. I stretched and yawned and wondered why I felt like I'd spent the night sleeping all folded up in a lawn chair. I opened my eyes and got the answer to that question. I turned to look at Steve. He was sound asleep — and he wasn't alone. Stretched out across his lap, eyes closed and purring like a miniature chainsaw was one small Willy/Billy cat with a belly that stuck out in all directions. Somehow, the T-bone had disappeared. All that was left was a piece of crumpled brown paper and a well-trimmed bone lying under the chair.

Sixteen

*S*teve was back at the Quarter Circle the next day — and back working horses the day after that, stiff, sore, and sour, but definitely in charge again. It was a good thing, because on Tuesday school started. There isn't much to say about that. What can you say about the beginning of another ten months of terminal boredom? As far as I could see, grade eleven was going to be the instant replay of grade ten, only more of it.

Raine and I were in the same class. That was about the only good news. We were both taking advanced diploma. She was taking it because she was smart and everybody in her family, including her, had always just naturally figured that was the way she was going to go. I wasn't quite sure why I was taking it. At the end of grade nine when the parents were supposed to decide with their kids which way to go, Pop had just shrugged and asked me what I wanted to do. I shrugged back and said that since I didn't figure on college or anything complicated like that I figured it would be a lot simpler just to take the easy stuff.

It was all settled until the day Pop had to go see the school counsellor about it — and he happened to meet Raine's mom in the hall. She'd been my grade eight teacher and was still suffering from the delusion that I had some brains if I cared to be bothered using them. She asked Pop what my plans were for high school and when she found out, she backed him into a corner and lectured him for about ten minutes on the importance of "challenging my potential" and all that other good stuff teachers use to mean they want some poor kid to suffer severely for the rest of his school career.

Well, Pop never has had any talent at managing women — especially when they're throwing big words at him. By the time he got out of that school I'd managed to bounce right out of auto mechanics and work experience and wind up submerged in French and biology. But it wasn't long after that when I discovered Raine — I mean, she'd been there all along but in junior high I was pretty ignorant when it came to anything but horses and football . . .

After that, I made sure I did enough work last year to *stay* in advanced diploma. Raine's mom thinks I've really learned to appreciate a proper education — but she always says that with a twinkle in her eye, so I'm not so sure who's fooling who.

Speaking of Raine's mom, Mary was home again the day before school. She took one look at Steve and asked him what he'd tangled with. He just looked her straight in the eye and, polite like he always is with her, said, "I had a little discussion with a man about a horse," and went on with what he was doing. Raine said Mary got the whole story out of her later and Mary's main comment had been that she was sorry Donovan was so long getting what was coming to him.

Pop phoned one night — from Dallas. He was at this guy's ranch, working on a saddle, and still having a pretty good time. I figured he was getting a little bit homesick, though. He said things were kind of domesticated there with the "over-the-hill gang" — none of which were any farther over the hill than he was, but I didn't tell him that. He said he'd be home before the snow flew — the way the weather in Alberta operates that could have been any moment — and then he asked to talk to Steve but he'd gone to town for groceries right then. Pop seemed a little bit concerned about not getting to talk to him. He stayed on the line for a while, talking about a lot of nothing at about five bucks a minute, which wasn't exactly logical, and then after an awkward pause, he asked, "How's he doin'?"

There was a pause on my end of the line. What did he want me to say? What could I say? Explaining how my brother was doing would take a lot more time than Pop had quarters — and it still wouldn't make sense. Besides, I thought, a little taste of bitterness welling up in my mind again, Pop ought to have all the answers. He was the one Steve told the big secret to the night he came. What did I know? I was just dumb little brother.

"He's okay," I said. "Gotta go, Pop, the bacon's burnin'."

My birthday rolled around. I celebrated it by failing a biology test, passing my driver's test, and pigging out on pizza — Raine took Steve and me out. Steve let me drive the Dodge to town — which I figured was birthday present enough from him, since he'd been flat broke ever since he bought the horse.

Then, instead of taking Raine back to her place, Steve

told me to turn in at our place. I did, and when we got out, Raine reached under the seat and came out with a big, lumpy package, wrapped up in birthday paper and tied with a bow. "Happy birthday, Beau," she said, and then, right there in front of Steve, she leaned over (yeah, it almost kills me to admit it but Raine's a couple of inches taller than me) and kissed me. Whoa! I figured sixteen was going to be the best year of my life!

Steve brought me back down to earth. "Well, Beauregard, you just gonna stand there with your face glowing like a bug zapper all night or are you gonna open your present?"

I gave him a foolish grin and opened the present. It was a bridle, hand-made with braided reins and little silver studs on the cheek pieces. Dad had made it last winter — and Raine had bought it from him in the spring. I'd always wondered why she never used it.

I didn't know what to say. It was beautiful, more than I'd ever expected, so what was the *one* thing I *did* manage to blurt out? "Geez, Raine, thanks. This is really great — except that I don't have a horse."

I could have strangled myself right then but Raine didn't even seem insulted. She just laughed. "You will sometime," she said. "Come on, let's go for a walk."

Obediently, I fell into step beside her. If she thought we should walk, we'd walk. I started to lay the bridle on the porch but she stopped me, "Don't just leave that lying around," she ordered. "Bring it along." I shrugged. Okay, we'd not only go for a walk, we'd take the bridle for a walk. Raine was a little crazy sometimes.

I wondered where Steve had disappeared to all of a sudden but I wasn't about to worry about it. Just Raine and me was kind of a nice change. But it didn't last. Just as we walked by the barn, the door opened and he came out.

He was leading Donovan's big, grey gelding. He'd kept the horse here ever since he got him, feeding him, grooming him, and taking real good care of him, but he never rode him. I'd been wondering what he was planning to do with him. Now I was about to find out.

He walked up to me and held out the halter rope. "Happy birthday, Beau," he said. For a minute I just looked at him. Finally I managed to spit out some words. "You're *giving* me the horse?"

Steve nodded. "Yeah. He goes with the bridle. You know, one of them package deals."

I looked at Raine. She was grinning. The two of them had been in on this together. But I still couldn't believe it was really happening.

"Hey, come on, Steve. You can't do this. This horse cost you over six hundred bucks — and a fair amount of blood. You can't just give him away for a birthday present."

Steve grinned. "Sure I can. I just did. I won't be around long enough to use him anyhow," he added, taking the bridle from me and turning away to slip it on the horse — and also, I think, so I wouldn't see the grin fade. "Just take good care of ol' Spook, huh, Beauregard," he said, his voice suddenly sounding kind of hollow. He handed me the reins, gave the grey a slap on the shoulder, and walked toward the house without looking back.

I stood there rubbing the horse's neck and remembering. Remembering the last grey horse I'd known called Spook. It had been so long ago I didn't think I even had it in my memory. The day of the auction sale at our ranch — when all the horses had to be sold because we were going to the city. I'd been too little to take in much of what was happening but one thing came back now, clear as yesterday. When Pop had to pry the reins out of Steve's hands so the new owner could take away his pony — Spook. It was the only time I could remember seeing Steve cry — until that first night he was here.

The big gelding nudged me with his soft nose. "Yeah, Spook," I said softly. "It's gonna be okay." And I wondered if I was telling the truth.

The Quarter Circle horse sale was set for the first week in October. That meant we all worked horses every spare minute from dawn to dark and then after dark in the lighted arena. A couple of times Raine and I managed to cut an afternoon of school to get in a little more riding time — but not both of us the *same* afternoon. Teachers have the instincts of bloodhounds when it comes to investigating simultaneous attacks of Friday-afternoon viruses.

But the second week in September Mary decided there was no way she could miss any more time at work, and since J.C. seemed to be getting better, she came home. After that, our school attendance took a real turn for the better and Steve ended up trying to do a three-person job by himself most of the time. He didn't seem to mind, though. I guess it was like he'd told me that time — working with horses was the only thing that made sense to him. But it wasn't just the horses he worked with. He did everything around the Quarter Circle that needed doing. Maybe if he worked hard enough and got tired enough he forgot whatever it was that haunted his sleep.

Actually, I was beginning to wonder if he ever did sleep any more. He was still using Pop's room and sometimes I'd get up and go to the bathrom way after midnight and the light would still be on and some rock station would be blasting heavy metal behind the closed door. A lot of mornings when I got up, he'd be already gone, over at the Quarter Circle and riding in the arena.

It was starting to wear him down — he'd lost weight so that my clothes he still kept wearing were actually beginning to fit him — and I figured he must be getting careless with the horses. A couple of times I'd come in after school to find him limping around with the knee ripped out of his (my) jeans or a big scrape up his arm. He'd just shrug and grin and say he'd had a "little wreck" with a horse but he'd never say which one. I couldn't figure it. All the sale horses were long past the bucking stage. But there was no point bugging him about it. Steve said exactly as much as he wanted and these days that wasn't much.

Anyway, I was having problems of my own. Spelled s-c-h-o-o-l. All the teachers I had seemed to have got involved in a competition over whose subject was most important and they went about proving it by seeing who could give the biggest pile of homework.

It was ten o'clock at night — about my usual time for finally breaking down and dragging out my books. For some reason Steve was feeling sociable for a change and he was sitting on the window bench with Willy/Billy perched on his shoulder and my guitar in his lap. For once he wasn't ripping its guts out with some hard rock song. He was just strumming softly and singing to himself real quiet. It was peaceful to listen to. Too peaceful, I thought, giving my head a shake. In another minute I was going to fall asleep and I *still* wouldn't have this stuff done.

My laid-back mood evaporated. I read the assignment for about the ninetieth time. Write a poem . . . Sure, lady, nothin' to it. I just whip off poems all the time. Me and Shakespeare, we're buddies.

I read the rest of the directions: ". . . a descriptive poem about some aspect of nature that has made a particular impression on you."

I stared at the blank paper. I couldn't do this. I mean, I like nature fine. Being outside. Feeling the sun and the wind. Feeling the silky power of a horse's muscles. Looking at the sky up there so big and empty. I can get pictures of it all in my head — but I can't turn them into a stupid poem.

But I had to try. So what was I thinking about? Oh, yeah, the sky. Well, here goes.

The sky above is very high . . .

Now, I've got to make it rhyme. (The teacher said it didn't necessarily have to rhyme but the last time I wrote an unrhymed poem she wrote on it, "Nice paragraph. Where's the poem?")

Okay, rhyming with high . . .

Big and blue, it fills my eye.

I groaned, mangled the paper, and threw it at the wastebasket. It missed and hit Steve. He stopped strumming and looked up at me with kind of a lazy-cat grin. "Somethin' itchin' you, Beau?" he asked.

I glared at him. "Yeah, somethin's itchin' me. And if you weren't so useless you'd stop pickin' and grinnin' and help me."

"Help you what?"

"Write poetry for my English class," I growled.

Steve sat up straight and looked mildly interested. "Poetry? No kiddin'? All they ever tried to teach me was nouns and verbs and stuff. Verbs are the ones that tell you who did it and nouns tell you what they did."

I just shook my head and didn't say a thing. Better teachers than me had tried to teach my brother grammar. It was obvious how far they'd got.

"So what you gotta write a poem about?" he asked, setting down the guitar and absent-mindedly scratching Willy/Billy's whiskery chops.

"Nature."

"You mean like the birds and the bees?" Steve asked with a wicked grin.

"No, I mean like the flowers and the trees."

He shrugged. "Doesn't sound so hard." He set Willy/Billy on the floor and wandered out of the room. So much for his help.

A minute later he was back. "Here," he said. I looked up just as he sailed a battered notebook across the room to me like a Frisbee. "Help yourself."

"What's this?" I asked, puzzled.

"What's it look like?"

I opened it up and flipped through the pages. They were all covered with writing — no, printing — some of the letter's a little off the regular shape, but real neat, like somebody had tried hard to make it perfect. It was all poetry. Some of it rhymed, some of it didn't. Some of it was hard and bitter, with titles like "Wino" or "Back Street," but some of *was* about seas and trees and skies. One title caught my eye. "You're Never Lonely." No way, I thought, everybody's lonely. I read it through . . .

> When you walk through the hills
> By the forrests and streams
> And know one is with you
> Just you and you're dreams

And the wild wind is blowing
In the tops of the trees
You can never be lonly
Just happy and free.
You can never be lonly
When you know you belong
Your a part of this big world
So young and so strong.

You can watch the rain falling
And night closeing in
Trees turning green
As thier new life begins
You can stand all alone
And watch the day end
And you don't need compannions
The earth is your friend
You can never be lonly
When you know you belong
Your a part of this wild world
So young and so strong.

You can walk in the city
With crowds all around
Where theres pavement and trafic
And loud city sounds.
The faces and voices and bodies arc there
But thats when you're lonly
Cause nobody cares.

I just sat there staring at the page for a minute. *That*
was *my* poem — the one I would have written if I could
figure out how to make a poem work. I understood it
like I'd never understood a poem before . . .

I looked up at Steve. He was watching me. "Who wrote this stuff?" I asked in kind of an awe-struck voice.

He shrugged and grinned kind of sheepishly. "*I* did. Who'd you think, Shakespeare? I thought you'd at least recognize the spelling."

"*You* write poetry?" I said in total amazement.

"Sure. Why not? Just 'cause I'm dumb don't mean I'm illiterate — or is that the other way around?" he said, his grin not quite hiding his embarrassment.

"Steve," I said softly, "this stuff is good." I found myself staring at him the same way I had that first night he'd come to the door.

I was seeing a total stranger again. A stranger who outran cop cars, out-fought Russ Donovan, bragged about hot-wiring cars and ripping off stereos — and wrote stuff that showed more soul and sensitivity than any lily-white A-student in Fenton High.

I paged through the book, glancing at lines and words, wanting to stop and read every page but curious about what all he'd written about. I was just about at the back when a loose page fell out. I picked it up. It was all creased like it had been crumpled up and smoothed out again. "Tracey," it said at the top. I started to read . . .

> When the world all turns cold
> And dark as a winter sea
> Living doesn't matter
> And your dying to be free
> Like dawn's first light
> She's at your side
> And makes you care again
> She'd got the strength to turn the tide . . .

I looked over at Steve again. He was just picking up the guitar. "Hey," I said, "Who's Tracey?"

The guitar slid to the floor, the strings giving out a mournful little sound when it hit. Steve slowly turned to face me. "What?" he said.

"Who's . . . ?" I began and, too late, realized that he'd heard what I'd said all too well. The next thing I knew he was across the room. His hand locked so hard onto the wrist of my hand that was holding the loose piece of paper that my fingers went numb and the paper floated down onto the bedspread. "Where did you get that?" he said in an almost-whisper that scared me worse than if he'd screamed the words at me. But in the same second that I got scared, I got mad. Ever since he'd walked in here I'd been living on a roller coaster. One minute he was helping me cheat on my homework, the next he was going psycho over nothing.

My eyes blazed right into his. "You gave it to me in the book with the others," I said, my voice slicing through the air as cold and deadly as that knife of his. "And for all I care you can take it and . . ."

All of a sudden he let go of my wrist, picked up the paper and tore it into a dozen pieces. He wadded them into a ball, threw them into the wastebasket, and ran out of the room and down the stairs. Second later I heard the roar of an engine and looked out the window just in time to see the Dodge go screaming out onto the main road and disappear like a solitary firefly into the blackness of the night.

So this is it, I thought. He drives in out of nowhere one night and drives out into nowhere another. And in between? And in between mostly all he did was mix up my life so bad I didn't know if I was coming or going.

So why did I stand there with tears stinging my eyes as I watched the red tail lights turn into tiny pinpoints that turned into nothing but darkness?

Seventeen

I got up at five the next morning — I might as well have got up earlier, I was awake all night — saddled Spook and rode him over to the Quarter Circle to help with morning chores. The horse was the only way I *could* get there, since all my reliable relatives had taken their vehicles and left the country.

Raine was just crossing the yard when I rode in. She gave me a thoughtful look. "Have a nice ride, Beau?" she asked, and I couldn't decide if she was being friendly or sarcastic. I knew I was late but I couldn't help it.

"Yeah, great," I muttered, getting down from Spook. I took a deep breath and got ready to break the news to her. "You're, uh, not gonna like this, Raine." I began walking beside her and leading the horse toward the barn. "But your horse trainer just up and left last . . ." We rounded the corner and there, behind the arena, the purple Dodge sat gleaming in the sunrise.

I stared at it. Raine stared at me. "Steve was already here working horses in the arena when Mom got up at six. He's about as sociable as an irritated bull moose and he looks like he hasn't slept all night." She took a closer look at me. "And so do you," she said accusingly. "What's going on over at your place anyhow?"

"I dunno, Raine," I said in a tired voice, and got started with my chores.

The day didn't get any better as it went on. In biology I fell asleep staring at an obscene picture of a frog without his skin on and by the time Mr. Milton got done taking a strip off me I wasn't too sure if *I* had any skin left.

In phys ed, I'd forgot to bring my gym shoes and shorts. I ended up playing touch-football in my riding boots and when I accidentally stepped on Jason Maxwell's finger he made such a fuss about it that I got sent to sweep the parking lot for the rest of the period.

Third period was English. I didn't have the poem done. Ms. Vance was "very disappointed in me." I was very disappointed in her. I thought she might have had a more forgiving nature.

Fourth period I spent in the counsellor's office — his idea, not mine — being yelled at by him and my teachers from the other three periods, with a special guest appearance from the principal himself. What they said filled up a lot of time but I can condense the message into five words. Shape up or ship out. But nobody really gave me the ship-out option. That made it even simpler. Shape up. Starting today, I was going to stay an hour after school every night working on homework until I had caught up on everything I was behind in and had brought my marks up to an average of at least seventy percent . . .

I managed to sneak out long enough after school to tell Raine I was going to be late getting to work — and why. She didn't say much but I could tell she wasn't exactly pleased. With the sale getting close we needed every possible minute with the horses. I knew she was thinking that she was spending just as much time working horses as I was and she still managed to get her homework done. But she was smart . . .

On my third day of detention good old Darcy Sanderson ended up in there with me. We've always had similar habits when it comes to homework. Now we were paying for our sins — along with about twenty other assorted sinners — under the cold eye of Mr. Pembrooke, the vice-principal.

After about half an hour, Pembrooke strolled out of the room — and the visiting began. Darcy, who talks a lot more efficiently than he works, filled me in on the most recent parts that had fallen off his TA, asked my opinion of the new redhead in grade ten, and then, out of the blue said, "Is your brother still around?"

"Yeah," I said. "He's working at the Quarter Circle. Why?"

Darch shrugged. "Just wondered. Guy was asking about him about at the service station yesterday."

I sat up straight and came to full consciousness. "Yeah? Who?" My first thought was that Russ Donovan was ready for round three.

"I don't know," Darcy said. He wasn't from around here. Drove a black Jag with B.C. plates and wanted to know if I knew Steve Garrett."

"What'd you say?"

"Well," Darcy said slowly, "this dude made me check the oil, put some air in a tire, and wash the windshield, paid for $19.50 worth of gas with a twenty-dollar bill, and then stood around waiting for the change and telling me to hurry up. So I told him I'd never heard of Steve Garrett."

"What'd this guy look . . ."

"Gentlemen!" Mr. Pembrooke's voice echoed across

the room. "You have already wasted too much time in socializing or you wouldn't be here now wasting my perfectly good afternoon as well as your own. Concentrate!"

I sighed and stared at my book — but I couldn't concentrate.

By the time we got out of there Darcy was already late for work, so all I got out of him was wave and "See you tomorrow!" as he raced out the door and spun the TA out of the parking lot in a spray of gravel.

I caught a ride to the Quarter Circle with a kid who was just going home from volleyball practice. All the way out there I thought about what Darcy had said. Steve and I were going to have a little conversation the minute I caught up to him.

I was just walking up the lane when I heard the most unholy commotion break out in the corral behind the arena. From the squealing and snorting and pounding of hoofs I figured there was one awesome horse fight going on back there. I dropped my books and took off running.

When I rounded the corner and caught my first glimpse of the corral, I still couldn't figure out what was going on. Raine was there, just standing on the second rail staring over into the corral instead of trying to do anything about whatever was going on in there.

Then I caught a glimpse of something through the corral rails. A horse. A jet black horse. And somebody in a red shirt was on the horse. The horse was Rebel. The shirt was mine. And the guy in the shirt was my brother. And what I'd been hearing wasn't a horse fight at all. It was a horse-human fight. Steve was trying to ride Rebel — and Rebel was doing his best to kill Steve for trying.

As I came up beside Raine I could feel the ground shake from the impact every time that horse went high in the air and landed with all four legs stiff as steel pipes. Every time he landed, Rebel gave a half-grunt, half-squeal, changed direction and went up again, twisting and sunfishing like he'd been born bucking. But Steve was staying with him. It was a fair fight and I wouldn't have put money on which one was going to win — until about the third time around the corral. That's when those pile-driver jumps started to loosen Steve up a little. I could see his reflexes were slowing down. He was reacting to the horse's moves instead of anticipating them. All of a sudden, Rebel swapped ends in the middle of a jump — went up going north, came down heading south, and unloaded Steve somewhere in the middle. Steve hit the ground hard and lay still for a few seconds. Then, moving like his bones were tied together with barbed wire, he slowly stood up, brushed a little dirt off himself, and limped over to where Rebel was standing, breathing hard and eyeing him warily. "Whoa there, you black-hearted outlaw," he said softly, gathering up the reins.

Raine climbed up another rail. "Come on, Steve," she called. "Quit while you're still ahead."

Steve turned to look at us. He was grinning like a little kid in Disneyland. "I ain't ahead," he said. "But I'm gonna be. Ol' Reb's gonna let me ride him this time, ain't you, Reb?" He was rubbing the sweaty, itchy spots on the horse's face, talking him down, getting ready to get back on.

I shook my head. "He's even crazier than I thought," I said. "Even he shouldn't need two lessons in one day to prove that horse is unridable."

Raine swung around to look at me. "Two?" she said. "Try four. Rebel already dumped him twice before you got here. And three times last night. I guess he was figuring on keeping this little competition a secret but I showed up when he didn't expect me so it got to be a secret for two.''

''Three now,'' I corrected. Steve edged the big black horse into a corner and slowly put a foot in the stirrup. Rebel didn't even twitch as Steve eased his other leg over and settled his weight into the saddle. ''Okay, Reb,'' Steve said softly, ''this time you're gonna be good, you listening to me?''

Rebel's ears were swivelled back toward Steve, not laid-back mad, just pointed back like maybe he really was listening. For a few long seconds the whole scene was motionless, like a freeze-frame from a movie, radiating with the tension of action held back. Then Rebel made up his mind. He *was* good — so good he unloaded Steve in six jumps this time.

I looked at my brother slowly picking himself up out of the dirt and then I turned to Raine. ''Why's he doing this?'' I asked.

Raine just shook her head. ''Why does Steve do anything?'' she said, but I thought I caught a little admiration sneaking in under the disgust in her voice. Then she was scrambling over the top rail and jumping down into the corral. I followed.

''That's enough for today, Steve,'' she said, all of a sudden in charge again.

Steve stood there thoughtfully rubbing his side — which was still probably only half healed from the fight — and looking at Rebel with more respect than I'd ever seen him give a human. Then he turned to Raine. ''Why, Raine? You figure Ol' Rebel's too tired to try again?''

Raine's eyes flashed dangerously. ''Rebel can go on chewing you up and spitting you out for the rest of the night without breathing hard,'' she said, ''but if he breaks your useless neck what are we supposed to do for a trainer? Get Russ Donovan back?''

Steve laughed, picked up the reins, and started leading Rebel toward the gate. ''Okay, boss, you win. Tomorrow's another day, ain't it Rebel?'' Then he glanced over his shoulder at me. ''Don't say anything to Mary about this until I get him broke, huh, Beau?''

I shrugged. ''Sure, Steve. I guess I can keep a secret for three or four years.''

Eighteen

*T*he rest of the day got even more complicated. A couple of prospective buyers came by to have a look at the horses and we ended up working half a dozen of them in the arena for them. That put us a couple of hours behind on the rest of the chores and then, just at dark, a neighbor phoned to say some Quarter Circle cows were out on the road, which led to an hour of fencing by the truck lights.

It was after ten when Steve and I got home. We flipped a coin for first turn at the shower and Steve won. He was out of there and in bed fifteen minutes later while I was still sitting at the kitchen table trying to memorize the digestive system of an earthworm for tomorrow's biology test. It wasn't till I finally hit the sack and was just drifting off to sleep that I remembered what Darcy had told me. My mind wanted to get up right then and go talk to Steve about it but my body refused to move.

The next thing I knew it was morning and I'd slept in, and all I had time to do was throw on my clothes and get in the car. But I had made up my mind to corner Steve tonight.

Things didn't turn out quite the way I had planned. It started out to be an ordinary enough day — nothing like a killer biology test to get the blood flowing first thing in the morning — and moved on through another three periods of normal drudgery. Things probably would have stayed normal if I hadn't run into a little good luck in detention, of all places. I had just settled down to endure another hour of torture when Mr. Milton came in, waving a paper of some sort, and proceeded to have a big pow-wow with Mr. Pembrooke. Then Mr. Pembrooke called me up to his desk. Great, I thought, now what have I done? What's the next penalty after a life sentence in detention?

My worst fears started coming true. It was my biology test that Mr. Milton had in his hot little hand. I stared at it, blinked, and stared again. The paper had my name on it but it couldn't be mine. There was a big red 78% at the top of the page. Mr. Milton was sort of squinching up his face into his best imitation of a smile.

"Well, Beau, I *knew* we could do it," he said, all excited. I just looked at him, wondering what the *we* had to do with anything. I hadn't noticed him sitting around here for an hour after school all week studying reproducing earthworms. I guess he took my lack of enthusiasm for modesty in the face of a compliment because he kept right on talking. "I've just been conferring with your other teachers and they tell me your homework is reasonably up to date, so —" he paused dramatically like he was about to announce the winner of an Academy Award "— I think it's only fair to excuse you from detention now."

Well, whoop-de-doo, I thought, wondering how to

thank him for such an honor, also wondering why he had to wait just long enough for me to miss the bus before he decided I didn't have to stick around.

Right about then I ran into another piece of good luck — about the last I was due to hit for a while. Just as I came out the door of the school I ran into Mary Kincade heading for her car. Getting a ride with her sure beat hitch-hiking, although I didn't particularly enjoy discussing with her the fact I'd been having a detention. We probably would have discussed it in more detail if she hadn't been rushing off to Calgary to visit J.C. tonight and just had time to dump me and two bags of groceries at the front door and take off again. I put the groceries away and headed out to the corrals to see what was happening.

As soon as I came around the corner of the barn I saw that Raine and Steve had Rebel out again. Raine was holding the bridle reins and Steve was putting the saddle on. Rebel was shifting around, restless as always, but he obviously didn't rate being saddled anywhere near as insulting as being ridden. "Stop your foolishness, you black-hearted devil." Steve's voice drifted across the barnyard, the words stern but the tone forgiving as it always was when he talked to Rebel.

Then Raine's voice: "He's not gonna let you ride him, Steve. When are you gonna get tired of getting bucked off and stomped on and give up?"

Steve laughed softly. "I'm not gonna give up. Not until I win."

"Or you get yourself killed."

Steve finished tightening the cinch and turned to look at Raine, his back still toward me. "Would it make any difference to you if I did?" he asked, his voice suddenly gone serious.

I knew what Raine's next move would be. She'd toss

her head and laugh and say, "Not really. But just don't do it before the horse sale, okay? We don't have time to find a replacement."

But she didn't laugh. There was a long pause and then she spoke in a voice so low I would have missed the words if I hadn't been close by then. "Yeah, Steve," she said, "it would make a big difference."

For a few long seconds they just stood there, staring at each other, and I just stood there, on the other side of the fence, staring at them. Some instinct told me that it would be a real good idea for me to yell, "Hi, there, what's happenin'?" or cough or start whistling Dixie or something. But I didn't. Maybe I had some self-destructive desire to see what would happen next.

Steve took a step forward and the next thing I knew Raine was in his arms and he was kissing her — and her arms were around him too, and she sure wasn't doing anything to discourage him. This was Raine who, a few short weeks ago, had belted him in the face for dragging her out of the way of getting trampled by Rebel. Raine, who I'd been stupid enough to think was *my* girlfriend? Who in all the time we'd been hanging around together had kissed me twice — once under the mistletoe at the school Christmas dance and once on my birthday. Things were changing fast around here. No, maybe they weren't changing at all. Maybe I was finally just seeing them the way they really were.

About a million thoughts were racing through my mind. The first and strongest was to charge in there and have a shot at rearranging my brother's face. I took a step forward — and then stopped. What was the use? Even in my wildest dreams I knew I couldn't beat Steve in a fight. Suddenly all I wanted was to get out of there — get as far away as I could. But I'd waited too long. Even as I started to turn away I saw Steve look up — and catch my movement from the corner of his eye. "Beau, wait!" I heard him call after me. But I was already running across the barnyard. I didn't look back.

I ran until I couldn't run any more. Then I walked. And I didn't stop until I got home. Then I almost threw some clothes together and took off down the road. Almost. That's what Steve would have done — that's what he *did* seven years ago. Hit the road and didn't look back. But even as the idea of doing it now crossed my mind, I knew I wouldn't. Not me. I had too much sense. I'd stick around. I always had — and look where it'd got me.

After about an hour of pacing around the house like a tiger in the zoo I finally flopped down on the couch, turned on the TV, and stared blankly at it for the rest of the evening. It was ten o'clock when I turned it off and I couldn't remember a thing I'd seen. I went up to my room and closed the door. There was no point in going to bed. I wouldn't sleep anyway. But there was no way I was going to be around downstairs when Steve came home — if he came home — so I just lay on the bed and stared into the darkness.

It was only a few minutes later that Steve drove in. I didn't look out the window but I knew it was him. That Dodge had a real distinctive sound to it. I heard the door open downstairs. "Beau? You home?" Steve's voice echoed through the house.

Footsteps through the house. "Beau?" He started up the stairs. "Oh, come on, Beau, don't do this to me, kid."

Do what, Steve? I thought bitterly. What's the matter? You finally develop a conscience at this late point in life?

The footsteps stopped outside my door. "Beau? I know you're in there. Open the door." I heard him trying to open the door but he was out of luck. It was locked. "Beau, open it or I'm gonna bust it."

"Go away!" I yelled, grabbing my riding boot from beside the bed and heaving it at the door as hard as I could. It hit with a satisfying thud but the sound was almost lost in a splintering crash that came a second later. The next thing I knew the light was on and Steve was standing in the doorway.

"Now," he said, "we're gonna talk."

I stood up. "Oh no, we ain't. I got nothin' to say to you." I started go around him but he grabbed my arm and threw me back onto the bed. That did it. I bounced back up and went at him, fists first. I swung and felt a pleasurable sting as my fist connected with his jaw. He staggered back a step, shook his head like he was clearing out the fog, and then just stood there looking at me. That threw me off completely. I'd expected to get hit back real fast. "Okay," Steve said, with a half-grin as he wiped a trickle of blood from his lip with his fist, "maybe I had that coming'. Now quit while you're still ahead."

"You've got a lot more than that comin'," I said, and went for him again. But this time, before my fist could connect, his hand locked on my wrist and he forced me back against the wall.

"Look, Beau," he said, breathing hard. "You're gonna listen to me. You can either do it now, the easy way, or I can pound on you till you're too tired to give me any more trouble. Which is it gonna be?"

I glared up at him, mad enough to spit — I might as well have done it. He was holding me so I couldn't do anything else to him. "So what big news are you gonna tell me, huh, Steve? That I imagined what I saw this afternoon?"

A muscle tightened in his jaw and his eyes wavered

ever so slightly. "No," he said. "You didn't imagine it. But I wish you had."

"What's that supposed to mean?"

Steve sighed and I felt the pressure on my wrist let go. He stepped back and I guessed he'd decided I wasn't going to try to kill him after all. He might have been wrong . . .

I peeled myself away from the wall and stood there rubbing circulation back into my wrist. "Look, Beau," Steve said, pushing his hair out of his eyes and turning to pace restlessly around the room, "I know how you feel about Raine. I didn't mean to hurt you. I didn't mean for this to happen."

"Yeah, sure you didn't, Steve," I said, my voice sounding loud and ragged in the small room. "It wasn't your fault, was it? You can't help being older, and taller, and better looking, and driving a hot car, and being just naturally irresistible. It never was much of a contest, was it? I was just good ol' Beau. Just the kid next door that was okay to hang around with till somebody real came along. And too dumb to know any better . . ."

Steve swung around to face me. "Don't start blaming it on Raine," he said, his voice low but his eyes dangerous.

I returned the look with equal voltage. "I'm not blaming Raine. I'm not even blaming you — even if you are the scuzz-bucket of the century. I'm blaming me for sitting around here all wide-eyed and innocent, trusting everybody in the whole world — including you. I should have grown up a long time ago. I should have been more like you."

For a minute, Steve just stared at me. The fire died out of his eyes and he suddenly looked different than I'd ever seen him. Younger, I think, like for once in his life he was scared. And yet older, too, as if he was too tired to fight any more. "No, Beau," he said in a voice suddenly gone tired too. "You shouldn't have been like me. Not ever."

He turned and started to walk out of the room but the anger inside me was still too strong to let him go. "Well, you don't need to worry about me, Steve. I'm not gonna get in your way. You and Raine, that's okay with me. I won't be around the Quarter Circle any more. You can tell Mary I quit. She can mail the wages I've got coming. And you can have your horse back too. I don't want him."

Steve stopped walking. He turned around slowly to face me. "You know, Beau, you're right," he said, his voice gone hard, "you *do* need to grow up. Everything in the world that matters to Raine and Mary — and even old J.C., for that matter — is riding on that horse sale next week. You know as well as I do what it's gonna take to make it work. There's only three people who know those horses well enough to show them right — and, like it or not, you're one of them. But that doesn't matter to you, huh, Beau? Your feelings got hurt so you're just gonna slink away and sulk like a whipped dog and if the Quarter Circle falls apart so much the better. Well, that's not the way it works and if you weren't such a spoiled little brat you'd be able to see it for yourself. You owe the Kincades better than that. And if you could see past your insulted pride you'd know you owed yourself better too." He paused, turned to leave, and then shot one last unreadable look over his shoulder. "If quitting was that easy, I'd be outa here tonight," he said. He walked out of the room and slammed the door behind him.

I did a lot more hating than sleeping that night — and a lot more thinking than I wanted to. For the first time in my life, I was glad when the alarm finally went off. Feeling like I'd been dragged through a knothole, I got up and went through the motions of getting washed and dressed and fed, all the while staying as far away from Steve as possible. But when he got in the car to drive over for morning chores at the Quarter Circle, I was in the passenger seat, waiting.

Without a word passing between us, we drove over and went to work.

Nineteen

*I*t was weird how the three of us could do chores together and yet be so far apart. Steve and I had said all we had to say to each other last night, but a couple of times I caught Raine looking at me like she really wanted to say something. I just turned away. There was nothing she could say that I wanted to hear. Even Raine and Steve barely spoke to each other, which I found pretty funny considering how well they'd been getting along yesterday.

I went through the motions of school that day and the next few days like I was sleepwalking. The only noticeable thing that happened all week was when good old Darcy made some comment about me not paying much attention to Raine lately and I instantly swung around and punched him right in the teeth. Not being one to lie down and play dead, he punched me back and he and I returned to detention for a couple of days.

Then, as if life wasn't a total wreck already, the day before the sale, I came down with the flu. I barely made it out of biology class fast enough to avoid barfing on the cow eyeball I was supposed to be dissecting — no wonder I was sick. Somehow I got through the rest of the day at school and even went over to the Quarter Circle afterward. I was so sick I could hardly see straight, but there was so much to do that even a crooked-seeing person was better than nothing. Raine and Steve were busy putting some of their horses through their paces one last time, just to get that last bit of polish on them, but I stuck to helping Mary groom horses and clean tack. I was dizzy enough I wanted to stay kind of closely acquainted with the ground in case I needed to fall on it in a hurry.

I could feel Mary's eyes on me as I wove my way kind of unsteadily around a horse I was brushing. At last she stopped combing the knots out of Arizona's tail, set down the comb, and looked at me the way she did back in grade eight when she was pretty sure I was the one that shot the spitwad. "Beau Garrett," she said firmly, hands on her hips, "are you sick?"

I gave her a bleary-eyed look, wiped the sweat off my face with the rag I'd been polishing the horse with, and finally managed to gulp, "Yes, ma'am."

She came over and felt my forehead. "I'll say you are. You're burning up. I should have known you were coming down with something. You haven't been yourself the last few days."

"Yes, ma'am," I said, not too sick to keep her sniffing down the wrong trail. "I've been gettin' sick all week."

She slid her arm around my shoulders. "Well, come on. We're going to get you inside and lying down before you fall down."

I shook my head. "No, I'm okay. There's too much work to do. I can . . ."

"Shut up, Beau," Mary said firmly. "I'm the

teacher." She started walking me toward the house and I suddenly realized how bad I wanted somebody to just take care of me for a change. I leaned against her shoulder and closed my eyes.

I hardly even remembered getting there, but the next thing I knew I was lying in Mary's spare bedroom with my boots off and a cool rag on my forehead.

I guess I spent the next couple of hours in a half-world between waking and sleeping. I know Mary came in a few times. Once she made me drink some ginger ale. I guess Steve and Raine came in the house for supper. I heard voices in the kitchen. The next time I woke up, all three of them were in the bedroom, looking at me. "You okay, Beau?" Steve said, looking real worried. What'd he think, he was the only indestructible Garrett on earth? I glared at him as hard as I could, which was only partly successful, since I kept seeing two of him. "Yeah," I growled. "Get outa here and leave me alone." I closed my eyes again, since that was the fastest way I could think of to get him out of my sight.

I guess they all figured I was unconscious or something because a big discussion about me sprang up right then. "I don't know," Mary said, her voice concerned. "He's pretty sick to leave here alone."

Steve's voice: "Yeah, maybe I better stick around until you and Raine get back."

That was just what I needed, being babysat by Steve. It made me mad enough to open my eyes again and sit up. "Look, I ain't *that* sick. Go run your errands and let me get some sleep. That's all I need."

They all looked at me and then at each other. Steve shrugged. "He's all right," he said to Mary. "You and Raine go ahead and take those papers in for J.C. to sign and pick up those extra saddles you're borrowing on the

way home. I can run into Olds and pick up the sale cata-
logues and still be back in less than an hour.''

''Well, okay, I guess that's how we'll have to do it,''
Mary said, still a little doubtful. ''You don't move out
of that bed, you hear, Beau?'' I muttered something and
closed my eyes.

I was still awake to hear the door close and some vehicles start up. That was the last I remembered — until
I heard an engine again. That hour had gone by fast.

Then someone was knocking on the front door. I
groaned. Company was all I needed. I wanted to play
possum so they'd think there was no one home and go
away. But what if it was some big-time buyer coming
early to ask about a horse? I'd better go see. I hauled
myself out of bed and checked myself over, relieved to
see I was wearing all my clothes except my boots and
shirt. The shirt was hanging on the doorknob so I
grabbed it on the way past and staggered into the hall-
way. I mean staggered. Getting up that fast when you're
kind of light-headed anyway can be hazardous to the
health.

I flung open the door and stood there staring stupidly
at someone I'd never seen before. A guy about thirty,
maybe, dark and kind of good-looking in a slimy sort
of way. I was instantly sorry I'd made the effort to get
up. This guy, in his sports coat and his shiny, expensive-
looking shoes, was not the horse-buying kind. ''Yeah,''
I said, feeling too lousy to be polite. ''What do you
want?''

He ran his eyes over me — I think. He was wearing
sunglasses, which I figured was pretty unnecessary, since
the sun had been down for half an hour. ''Who are
you?'' he asked.

Well, I didn't need to worry about being polite. This
guy had less manners than I did. I gave him kind of an

insolent stare and then, maybe because I was too sick to think fast I answered the question. "Beau Garrett. Who are you?"

He ignored my question. He just studied me some more from behind those impenetrable glasses. "You're Steve Garrett's brother." It was a statement, not a question, and it cleared my head like a good gulp of drain cleaner. I glanced over to where his car was parked. It was black — a Jag with B.C. plates. Somebody else, a big guy, was sitting in the passenger seat, but I couldn't see his face.

"So," I said belligerently, "what if I am?"

"I want to talk to him," the guy said coolly. "Where is he?"

I managed a laugh and an arrogant shrug that was just about the way Steve would have done it himself. "Beats me," I said. "Try California. That's where he said he was goin'."

The guy suddenly tensed. If he'd been a horse he would have pricked up his ears. Slowly, he took off the glasses. I wished he'd have left them on. His eyes were just as cold and empty without them. "What?" he said.

"You heard me. My good old reliable brother had a fight with the boss lady this afternoon, and just like that, he up and quit, threw his stuff in his hot purple car and drove off, leaving Kincade's without a trainer to show their horses at the big sale tomorrow. My brother's a real nice guy." I managed to get the right degree of hate into that last line without much trouble at all.

"What makes you so sure it's California?"

"Sure? I ain't sure of nothin' about Steve. But when he picked up his back pay he just looked out the window and hollered. 'Have fun, suckers! While you're shovelling snow this winter I'm gonna be on the beach at Malibu.' " I paused and gave the stranger a thoughtful look. "What do you want him for anyhow?"

"It's personal," he growled back.

"Well, if it involves damaging his face, hit him once for me too."

The stranger gave me a smile that would have looked better on a shark. "I'll keep that in mind," he said. He gave me one last, penetrating look, turned and walked over to the car. As he drove away, I got a look at the guy in the passenger seat. Russ Donovan.

I stood there leaning on the porch railing and it suddenly occurred to me that I was shaking all over. Some instinct was telling me that this guy played in a whole different league than I understood. That behind those cold glasses and colder eyes was somebody that gave a whole new meaning to the word "bad."

Dizzily, I went back inside, shut the door, and for a minute, just stood there leaning against it and wondering if I was delirious and had imagined the last few minutes. I wished I had been. But I knew it was real. Too real. I went into the kitchen, sat down at the table, and laid my head on my arms, trying to think.

Twenty

*I*was still there half an hour later when Steve came in.

"Hey, Beau, how you doin'? You're supposed to be . . ."

"Get in here, Steve."

Steve gave me a puzzled look. "I was plannin' on it," he said. "Just as soon as I could get through the door. You don't look too good, Beau. Maybe you better . . ."

"Shut up and listen. I've got some questions and you better have some answers, right now."

Steve came into the kitchen. "What's goin' on?"

"Friend of yours was here askin' about you," I said, and watched as the color drained from his face.

"What?"

"Dark hair, dark eyes, five-ten or so, about thirty, comes from B.C. That ring any bells?"

Steve stared at me for a long time, almost like a wild animal caught in the glare of headlights. Finally he nodded. "Yeah," he said softly. "Where is he now?"

"On his way to California if you're lucky," I said, and explained what I'd told the guy.

A crooked smile flashed across Steve's face. "You're a better liar than I figured," he said. "Thanks, Beau, I owe you one."

I didn't return the smile. "You owe me a lot more than that," I said through my teeth. "You owe me an explanation about what's been going on around here for the past month and you might as well get started now because neither of us is moving until I hear it. You can start with what you did that brought you running to Fenton and your ever-loving family with a pocket full of money and an allergic reaction to the sight of a cop. And then you can move on to a few other details — like who Tracey is . . ."

At the mention of that name, something close to physical pain flickered across my brother's face, but all I felt was satisfaction. At least he knew what it felt like to get hurt.

Steve shook his head. "It's a long story, Beau."

"Then you better start now 'cause I'm gonna hear it all and I'd rather hear it before Raine and Mary get back. Start at the beginning. Why'd you run away in the first place? Didn't you figure Pop had it bad enough? First he loses the ranch, then Mom takes me and pulls out, and then you had to go and run out on him."

Steve had lit a cigarette and was standing staring out the window. Now he turned around and looked at me. "It was either run or get put in a foster home," he said, low-voiced.

"What do you mean?"

"I got in a bunch of trouble at school one day and Pop had to come down to see the principal. And he showed up drunk . . ."

"You're lying! Pop don't even drink."

"He don't now. And he didn't before Mom took you and left. You don't know what he was doin' after that. I don't think he knew half the time either.

"Anyhow, there was a big commotion at school and then that night a social worker came to the house. I sat in the bedroom, listening through the door. Most of the conversation wasn't all that hard to hear — and it didn't take a genius to figure out that some big shot had decided Pop wasn't being a responsible parent. When the social worker started making noises about a foster home, I took thirty bucks out of Pop's dresser, threw some clothes in a bag, and crawled out the window.

"I started hitch-hiking, heading either west or south. I didn't care where I went as long as it wasn't too cold. The first ride was going west so I headed for Vancouver. Figured things couldn't be any worse there than they were at home."

"Were you right about that?"

He studied his cigarette. "No," he said, real quiet. "I almost starved to death the first couple of months — till I learned what places put out good garbage — and I learned how to steal. Whatever it took to get something to eat, I did. There's only two things I didn't do. One was beg and the other . . ." His voice trailed off, and for once, I didn't ask. "I finally fought my way into a gang. Took me a long time to get accepted. They were mostly Asian kids, Vietnamese. I learned a lot about survival from them. We ripped stuff off, but the easiest money from making deliveries."

I stared at him. "You mean delivering drugs?" I asked, feeling like this was some movie he was telling me about.

"Yeah."

"What kind of drugs?"

Steve shrugged. "Does it matter? Anything illegal. All the way from grass to crack."

"And I guess you had a few free samples along the way, too, huh?"

Steve's eyes met mine. "I guess so."

"So all that stuff you said about working with horses out there was a lie."

"No, it wasn't," Steve said quickly, like it was real important that I believe him about this. "When I was about fourteen, one of the guys I used to make deliveries to turned out to be the owner of a racing stable. One day I heard him complaining about not being able to find any kids who could handle horses for stable boys and I figured, why not? It couldn't be any worse than the way I was living so I went to work for him."

"So," I said sarcastically, "at the ripe old age of fourteen you actually went straight?"

Steve shook his head. "Not exactly. I worked hard and did what I was told and finally worked my way up to jockeying for him on some of the 'B' tracks out there. He wasn't hard work for — as long as you did things the way he wanted them done. Including losing the races he wanted you to lose. I hated that part. Not on account of the people that got burnt betting on fixed races. They were taking their chances. But it wasn't fair to the horses. Especially this one big black horse named Tarpot. He'd been brought up from the States somewhere and he was wiping up the 'B' circuit. He was the best horse I ever rode. Won ten races in a row and the boss figured there'd be enough money riding on his next race to be worth betting against him. So I got the order to pull him up. I was gonna do it. I'd done it on enough other horses. We were ahead by half a length on the far turn when I started pulling him up. But when Tar saw that first horse start to pass him, he just about went crazy. I never saw a horse fight like that. He almost pulled my arms out of their sockets but I managed to hold him till two more horses went by. The leader was into the home-stretch so I figured that I could let him go a little. Well, as soon as he felt the reins loosen he gave a leap like he was just comin' out of the gate and started gaining again like those other horses were standing still. I could have pulled him in again, but all of a sudden, I had to let him have his chance. I had to find out just how much heart that horse really had. I gave him his head and rode him like I'd never rode any horse before. He passed the third, the second, and it was a photo for first. Tar won. And it was the last race I ever rode.

"I found out later that the boss lost fifty thousand dollars on that race. He told me that just before he and two other guys dragged me out behind the barn and beat me unconscious. I woke up the next day in an alley, out of a job, broke, and too busted up to work. I could only think of one thing to do . . ." His voice trailed off.

"So you went back to your old job pushing dope," I finished for him.

He nodded. "Yeah. Pushing it, taking it. It didn't much matter. I'd had my shot at making it doing some-thing I cared about and after that blew up in my face, nothing much mattered. At least if I stayed high most of the time I didn't have to think too much."

"Didn't it ever occur to you to just come home?"

"Home to what? I phoned once. The operator said the number wasn't in service. Anyway, after leaving the way I did, there was no way I could come crawling back home broke and desperate and expect Pop to take me in."

That kind of stubborn pride was pure Steve, all right. But I figured it *was* desperation that finally brought him back — even if he wasn't broke any more. I decided to let that part go for now. I had a more important question.

"Who's Tracey?"

The pain slid across Steve's face again. He turned away and stared out into the darkness. "Tracey saved my life," he said in a voice that didn't sound like Steve.

There was a long silence. A wrong word now and I knew I'd never hear the story. Steve walked over to another window and stood there looking out like there was something in the darkness that only he could see.

"Tracey was a waitress," he said at last. "She worked in a little greasy spoon where I used to hang out a lot. She wasn't from Vancouver either. Maybe that's why we used to talk to each other. She was from a little town outside Kamloops. She liked horses. Used to barrel race back there. She had a baby."

I was staring at Steve wide-eyed now, trying to fit all the disjointed pieces of the story together — and coming up with the obvious answer. I guess he could practically hear the wheels going around in my head because he suddenly looked at me and laughed. "Don't go gettin' any ideas, Beauregard. She had the baby before I even met her. That's why she ran away from home. Couldn't stand to tell her parents she was pregnant — and of course the loyal boyfriend left town when he heard the good news.

"So there she was alone in Vancouver, trying to support herself and a kid on a waitress's pay. And she was doing it, too. I don't know how but I'll guarantee you every buck was honest money. That's the way she was, honest and strong." He took a sudden deep breath, turned away, and wiped his sleeve across his eyes, and for the first time, it hit me that maybe I *didn't* want to hear the rest of this story. But I knew I had to.

"How'd she save your life?" I asked.

"I told you I was doing drugs a lot by then. I guess the truth is I was an out-and-out junkie. Messing around with so much different stuff it's funny I'd stayed alive that long. I was in too deep to even care by then. But Tracey cared. She stuffed me in cab one day when I was too wired to know what she was doing, dragged me off to this de-tox centre, told 'em I was her brother and she was signing me in there. By the time I got straight enough to realize what she'd done, it was too late to get out. I could have killed her. I probably would have if I could have got hold of her. Until I realized that she hadn't just dumped me there. She came to see me every day after work. Some days they wouldn't let her see me but she always came.

"I spent four months of hell in that place, but when I walked out of there, I knew two things. I'd never do dope again — and I was in love with Tracey." Steve's voice went ragged and he took a few deep, shaky breaths before he could go on.

"We were gonna get married. Yeah, I know we were too young — I was eighteen and she'd just turned nineteen — but we figured we'd grown up a little faster than most. We were gonna get out of the city, find a place were we could work with horses. Some day we were gonna get a place of our own." He stopped talking, and for what seemed like forever, the only sound was the clock ticking away.

I couldn't stand the silence. "What happened, Steve?" I asked, almost reluctantly.

"I ended up in jail," Steve said, the words coming out blunt and bitter. "Tracey begged me not to do any more drug deals. And I wasn't going to. But Romero — " A sudden shiver ran up my spine as I recognized the name, the one that Steve had yelled out in that nightmare the day of the fight with Donovan.

"Romero came around to see me, offered me a thousand dollars just to pick up a package off a fishing boat and deliver it to another guy. A thousand dollars would have gone a long way to get me and Tracey out of Vancouver, only I never got the thousand. I handed the package to an undercover cop who'd been trying to bust Romero for a long time. I wasn't the one they wanted. They didn't have enough evidence against me for much of a charge so I wound up doing six months. It should have been nothing. It *was* nothing, except . . ." Steve's voice faltered and something close to a sob shook his body, "except Tracey was left on her own. She came to visit me in jail for the first couple of months and then she sent a note that she was sick and couldn't make it. I was going crazy worrying about her. But then Romero came to see me."

"He came to jail?"

"Sure, why not? He didn't have anything to worry about. I was the one that got caught. I took the rap. He was clean. But he was gonna help me out. He was gonna keep an eye on Tracey . . ." Suddenly, Steve slammed his fist against the wall. "Yeah, he looked after her."

Steve's voice was shaking now but he kept on talking. "I finally got out on day parole. I was just about crazy by then. I hadn't heard from Tracey for nearly a month. I went to the café where she worked — and found out she'd been laid off for nearly six weeks. Nobody knew where she was. I went the only other place I could think of. To the old Chinese lady that looked after the baby for Tracey. As soon as the door opened, I heard the baby crying and I just about passed out from relief. If he was still here, Tracey wasn't gone. Everything was okay.

" 'Where's Tracey, Ming?' " I said, and I'll never

forget the look on Ming's face. For a minute, she didn't say a word but her eyes filled up with tears and I felt the bottom drop out of my world. 'You don't know, Steve?' she whispered, and I could only shake my head.''

Steve was crying now, unashamedly.

"She was dead, Beau," he said, his voice a choked whisper. "You know how she died?"

I just shook my head.

"Cocaine. Tracey, who never did dope in her life, died of a cocaine overdose. Ming found out. She's got connections. And you know where Tracey got it?"

"Romero?"

"Yeah. My friend, Carlos Romero."

"But why? You mean he killed her deliberately? Or he got her the coke and she killed herself?"

Steve shrugged. "I never really found out. The way Ming got the story it was an accident. Romero uses the stuff all the time, and supposedly he talked her into trying some just to make her feel better about losing her job and everything. I heard at the de-tox center that once in a while a person has a violent reaction to coke, and in a matter of seconds, they're dead."

"You believe that's what really happened?"

Steve shook his head. "I don't know. I'll never really know." Then he raised his head and the anger in his eyes blazed through the tears. "But it doesn't matter, 'cause I do know for sure that Romero gave her the coke. He killed her."

"What'd you do when you found out?"

"Got drunk out of my mind — and got myself a gun. I knew I was gonna kill Romero, but before I knew it, I was too drunk to see straight, let alone shoot straight. When the bars closed I took another bottle and headed down to the beach to be by myself. I guess I finally passed out down there because I woke up in the morning alone on a deserted stretch of beach. I recognized the place. Tracey and I used to walk there all the time. That's when losing her really hit me. I cried my guts out there for hours, just me and the sand and the sea gulls — and I also sobered up. And by the time I was finished. I knew that, however bad Romero deserved to die, I wasn't gonna kill him. Not for Tracey. Because to murder somebody for her would be like spitting on everything she cared about. If I ever had any good in me, Tracey found it. She believed in me, more than I'd ever believed in myself. Every time I closed my eyes I could see her face and I knew she'd forgiven me for a lot of things but she'd never forgive me for killing somebody.

"But I still was gonna make Romero pay. And then I thought of the perfect setup. I knew Romero's operation inside out. And I also knew that one of those Crime Stoppers organizations was offering three thousand dollars to find out how these big shipments of coke were getting into the city." An expression of grim satisfaction crossed Steve's face. "So I called them up and told them when and where Romero's fishing boat met a yacht that brought a load of stuff up from Mexico every week, collected the money and the baby, broke parole, and got out of town."

"The baby?" I echoed.

Steve smiled. "Yeah, I took him to his grandparents. It was quite a trip. I never knew babies needed changing that often."

I couldn't help laughing. The idea of my outlaw brother driving halfway across B.C. in his hot purple car with a howling baby in the front seat and a back seat full of Pampers was more than I could believe. "Did his grandparents even know the kid existed?" I asked.

"Yeah, Tracey wrote to them a while back and told

them the whole story. We'd been going to go visit them. They'd been going crazy wondering what happened to the baby after . . .'' His voice broke. "After they got the phone call from the cops about Tracey being dead.''

"And then you headed over here to hide out?''

Steve nodded. "Yeah. I'd managed to track Pop down by writing to an old friend of his that knew where he'd gone. I'd been gonna come home and bring Tracey and . . .'' This time, Steve didn't fight back the sobs. He just sank into a chair and laid his head on his arms and cried like a baby. It was the first time in my life that I didn't feel a million years younger than him.

Hardly realizing I was doing it, I stood up, went over, and laid my hand on his shoulder. "It's gonna be okay, Steve,'' I said softly wishing for all the world I was telling the truth.

Some time passed. Steve stopped crying and just sat there silently, his face buried in his hands. I stood there, wondering what somebody less stupid than me would do or say right now. I wished Pop was home. Or Mary? No. Not Mary. This was Garrett business. It stayed in the family.

"Steve?'' I said at last.

He looked up at me.

"What are we gonna do now?''

Steve wiped a sleeve across his wet face. "We?'' he said, his voice steady again and a ghost of his old taunting grin playing across his face. "Isn't this the scene where the Lone Ranger asks Tonto, 'What are we gonna do?' when they're surrounded by five hundred war-painted Apaches and Tonto says, 'What do you mean *we*, white man?' You don't have to do anything, Beau. I dealt the cards, it's up to me to play the hand.''

I shook my head. "Wrong, as usual, Steve. You're my brother. Deal me in.''

Twenty-one

Steve and I went home. We made quite a pair heading out to the truck — the walking wounded. Me still so light-headed from the flu that I had to remember not to lean forward too far in case I just kept on going till I did a face-plant on the ground, and Steve so drained he was like a walking zombie.

The cool night air did a lot to clear my head. By the time we got home I was beginning to feel like I might live after all, but Steve made me go straight to bed. "Steve?" I said as he pulled the blanket up over me, "you're gonna wait till I go to sleep and then take off, aren't you?"

He gave me a long, thoughtful look that I couldn't read and then shook his head. "Uh-uh, Beauregard, I ain't goin' nowhere. I got a horse sale to run tomorrow, remember?"

I stared at him. "But what about Romero?" And then I remembered something I hadn't told him. "Russ Donovan's with him too."

Steve gave a low whistle. "Now there's a happy couple. Maybe we'll get lucky and they'll kill each other and relieve the world of two problems at once. Anyhow, they went to California, remember?''

"Maybe," I said doubtfully.

Steve pulled a chair up beside the bed and sat down.

"Get some sleep, Beau. We'll sort out tomorrow in the morning. I'll still be here." Then with a grin he added, "Trust me."

And the weirdest part was, I did. But I didn't go to sleep. Not for a long time. We talked. About everything. About how the bust he set up for Romero worked — except that, as usual, Romero himself managed to slide out through a crack in the system. A good lawyer and he was out on bail — and on Steve's trail — in twenty-four hours.

He talked about Tracey some more. And this time it didn't seem to hurt so much. "Here," he said at last, pulling his wallet out of his back pocket and handing it to me folded open, "it's about time I showed you this." The picture was worn around the edges, like it had been handled a lot, but the face was still clear. For a minute I thought it was Raine's face but then I knew I was wrong. The hair was Raine's, that great, one-in-a-million strawberry-blond color. The eyes could have been Raine's, except that they were blue. And the smile, that sassy you-name-it-I-can-do-it grin, was pure Raine. But the face wasn't Raine's. It was a little older, a little thinner, and a little harder. It was Raine a few years down the road — if those years turned out to be hard ones.

Slowly I looked up at Steve. "Do you understand now, Beau?" he said softly.

Did I? For some long seconds my brother and I searched each other's faces. Finally I nodded.

"So, you gonna keep the horse?"

It took a minute for me to figure out what that question had to do with me understanding. But then I realized what it had to do with was forgiving. Accepting Steve's present was accepting Steve.

I made up my mind. "What do you think? I'm gonna give up the best — not to mention only — horse I ever owned? You think I'm stupid or something?"

Steve's old wicked smile was back. "In answer to your question, Beauregard, yes, but I'm glad you're keeping Spook."

I half sat up, considering taking a swing at him, got dizzy and flopped back on the pillow.

"You always swore you were gonna get the other Spook back," I said softly.

Steve smiled and shook his head. "Yeah, when you're ten you think you're gonna do a lot of things."

"Things would have been a lot different if we could have kept the ranch," I said sleepily.

"Don't start thinking 'ifs,' Beau. It'll drive you crazy . . ."

I didn't. I dreamed them instead. All night long I dreamed about being a little kid again, back when we had a ranch and a family, before things went and got so complicated.

Twenty-two

*B*ut sometime later on, the dreams turned into a nightmare. A nightmare with a black car and a man with no eyes — only black holes that reflected the light. And Steve. Alone in the middle of an open field with the car screaming straight toward him. I had to save him. But I was frozen solid. I couldn't move. "Steve!" I was trying to scream, but even my voice was frozen . . .

Suddenly I was sitting bolt upright in bed staring at the numbers on the clock. Five forty-five. It was morning. Then I glanced at the chair by the bed — and knew the nightmare wasn't really over. Because Steve was gone.

The next thing I knew, I was out of bed and over at the window, staring out into the greying darkness. A huge surge of relief rushed through me. The Dodge was still in the driveway. I was half dressed before I realized something else. I wasn't sick any more. I bent over fast to pull on my boots, felt the floor give a minor lurch, and corrected that conclusion to I wasn't *very* sick any more. I went downstairs.

Steve was in the kitchen making coffee. "Hey, Beauregard. How come you're not sick in bed?"

"Can't be," I said. "We've got a horse sale to run."

Steve grinned. "You got it," he said. "Here, this'll clear the cobwebs out of your head." He handed me a cup of coffee that would have cleared all the smog out of Los Angeles. But I drank it — and when I didn't throw up I knew I really was cured.

I risked a piece of toast, half of which Waylon begged me out of, and watched as Steve actually straightened up the kitchen — living here in Fenton had really broke his spirit. Then he went upstairs and came back carrying the duffle bag he'd dragged into the kitchen that rainy August night.

I watched him, a lump slowly growing in my throat. "So you're really gonna do it," I said bitterly. "You're gonna finish your job at the Quarter Circle with the sale and then you're gonna run again."

Steve looked at me. "You know I don't have any choice."

I shook my head stubbornly. "There's a choice, Steve. You could call the cops. Tell them about Romero."

Steve just laughed. "Tell 'em what? That he's driving around Fenton asking questions about me? No law against that. They might get him on jumping bail, at best. They'd get *me* for parole violation and I'd be back in jail so fast it would make your head spin. No thanks." He pulled on his jacket and headed for the door. "Let's go. We got some horses to sell." He went out. I swallowed the last of my coffee and went to grab my jacket off the hook.

Just then the phone rang. I grabbed it. It was Pop.

He was back at Pincher Creek and chatty as all-get-out. "So what's happening up there, Beau? Have I missed anything important?"

A sudden blast of red-hot anger rushed through me. "Yeah, Pop. You've missed plenty and if you don't hurry up and get home in the next few hours you're gonna miss your oldest son for another few years — if he lives that long." I slammed the receiver back on the phone and ran out the door.

By noon we had everything ready. The auctioneer was there and all set up in the arena. The twenty sale horses, groomed till they shone, waited quietly in their stalls. Cars, trucks, and trailers were beginning to fill the hay-field parking lot as buyers and "lookers" drifted in.

The first horse to sell was Silverado, a flashy grey barrel-racing prospect that Raine had been working with. Raine rode him out, around the arena a few times, and then we set up the barrels and she did a run on him. He was fast and he slid around the turns like greased lightning. He was going to be a winner someday. A roar of approval went up from the crowd and the bidding started. When the auctioneer finally hollered "Sold!" it was a guy from Calgary whose fourteen-year-old daughter was nearly hugging him to death. I could almost have hugged him myself. He'd paid seventy-five hundred dollars. That was the way to start a sale!

And that was pretty well the way the sale went. Oh, there were a few little hitches. One horse pulled up lame at the last minute so we had to scratch him from the sale. Oh yeah, then there was the little incident with me and Arizona. We'd come a long way since that time he planted me firmly in the good old Alberta soil and now he was looking like a real good cutting-horse prospect.

I took him out in the arena with a bunch of cattle so the buyers could see him work. Unfortunately, they saw more than that.

At the rate we were switching saddles from horse to horse somebody had to make a mistake sometime. It happened with Arizona. Whoever saddled him didn't notice that the little strap that holds the back cinch to the front cinch had slipped off. Arizona made one fast turn and dive to turn back a cow, and the back cinch slid back till it grabbed him right around the flanks. That did it. Put a flank strap around any horse, and nine out of ten times, he's gonna buck. And Arizona wasn't one to go against the odds. Right there, in front of all those nice people, he decided to unwind.

This time, I *was* paying attention. We did a couple of very active trips around the arena before I got him sorted out and found out what had caused the whole wreck. The auctioneer explained to the crowd what had happened, Arizona snorted disgustedly a couple of times, we went back to cutting out cattle, and to my total amazement, the bidding took off again. Afterward, the guy who bought him came up to me and told me that if I could ride out that storm and get the horse calmed down and back to work that way, I could have a job at his ranch any day. That made me feel better than I had in a long time and I almost forgot all the thunderclouds hanging in the air.

The first one struck at intermission. I was in the office checking some stuff with Raine and Mary when the phone rang. Mary answered it. It was J.C. Mary listened, frowned, listened some more. "Are you sure, J.C.? We'll never get another one like him." More listening. The frown got deeper. "Maybe just another few weeks? I think he's starting to settle down. Maybe we should give him another chance." A lot more listening. A sigh. "All right. If you're sure that's the way you want it. Bye."

"What'd he say, Mom?" Raine asked.

"You're not going to like this much, honey," Mary said quietly.

"What?"

"Your dad wants me to sell Rebel at the end of the sale today," she said.

"Oh, Mom, you can't!"

"Yes, Raine, I'm afraid I can. You know your father's probably right," she said reluctantly. "That horse is just plain unmanageable." Mary turned to me. "Go tell Steve to get him ready please, Beau."

By the time I found Steve, the sale was starting again and he was already in the arena with a horse. I turned to go get Rebel myself but then I realized I had to show the next horse. "Hey, Sam," I yelled at a neighbor who'd been helping us bring horses in, "will you get the black stallion out of the barn? Watch him, he's a little rank."

Sam nodded. "I'll get him ready, Beau."

The first horse sold and Steve rode him out. We met in the gateway as I rode in. "Stick around," I said. "I've gotta talk to you."

Absent-mindedly, I put my horse through his paces, he sold, and I rushed out to find Steve. He was waiting just outside. "What's goin' on, Beau?"

"Rebel's goin' up for sale."

Steve stared at me. "Why?"

"Because J.C. phoned and said so."

"So J.C.'s gonna win," Steve said angrily. "He's crazy to sell that horse. Rebel's no outlaw. I'd have been ridin' him in a few more days."

"I thought you weren't figuring on being around in a few more days."

That comment hit home. Steve looked away. Then he sighed. "You got it, Beau. Let's go get the horse. The Quarter Circle's gonna get rid of two rebels in one day."

We were walking over to the barn when somebody called my name. I turned around. It was Darcy Sanderson, strolling around, looking at the horses. "Hey, Beau," he said. "Did you know your old man is back in the country? He just drove in."

Great timing, Pop, I thought. You got to the movie just in time to watch the cowboy ride into the sunset.

"Thanks, Darce," I said. "He'll find us if he wants to."

The barn door opened and out came Sam Clarke and Rebel — not necessarily in that order. Actually, Rebel kind of led Sam out. Sam's feathers looked a little ruffled. "White lightnin'!" he muttered, wiping a hand across his sweaty face. "Who's the lucky winner that gets to ride him in the ring?"

"Thanks, Sam," Steve said, laughing as he took the reins. "He ain't exactly broke to ride. I think the general idea was to sell him at halter."

"I can see why," Sam muttered, and hurried back toward the arena.

Then a thoughtful look came on Steve's face. He studied Rebel for a minute, glanced around the deserted back corral where we stood, and then grinned wickedly. "Well, since you're all saddled up, why not one last time, huh, Reb? Stand back, Beau, there could be a little action." He gathered up the reins and turned to get on.

"You can hold it right there, Stevie baby." The cold voice from behind me sent icy needles up my spine. I didn't need to turn around to know who it was but I turned anyway. Romero standing there with a short, black, deadly-looking pistol in his hand. Russ Donovan was beside him. "Told you he wouldn't cut out before the big sale," Donovan growled. "He had to stick around to take credit for training the horses *I* started."

Steve ignored Donovan and turned a cold, level stare on Romero. I could read a lot of things in my brother's eyes right then. Hate, contempt, disgust . . . But one thing I didn't see was fear. And somehow that just scared me more. Romero could kill Steve with a flick of his trigger finger, and at this moment, I wasn't so sure that Steve even cared.

"Well, Romero," he said. "Times must be gettin' hard. Since when did you start doin' your own dirty work?" He shifted his scornful gaze to Donovan. "Trust me, Romero, you could have found a better class of goon than this one. He and I have already tangled twice — and I won."

Donovan swore and took a step forward, but Romero stopped him. "No, not here." He motioned with the gun. "Come on, Garrett. Let's get out of here, nice and quiet, and nobody else will get hurt."

Before I had time to even wonder where I was going to fit in all this, Raine's voice broke into my thoughts.

"Steve! Beau! Where are you? The auctioneer's waiting."

I glanced over my shoulder to see her running toward us from the arena. There was somebody behind her but from this angle I couldn't see who. And suddenly it didn't matter who. Because right then I realized that Raine could be running right into the middle of a shooting. For a split second, Romero glanced in her direction too, and that was when I launched myself at him with that tackle I'd been practicing in phys ed all fall.

It worked! His knees buckled and he went down in a heap, the gun falling from his hand. "Get outa here, Steve!" I yelled.

For a second, he hesitated. Then he did something so crazy I couldn't believe I was seeing it. In one lightning move he had swung into Rebel's saddle. "Hee-aaa, Rebel!" he screeched, leaning forward in the saddle and touching his spurs to the big horse's sides. Rebel's ears shot straight up with surprise. He took a huge leap, landed stiff-legged, gathered his muscles and leaped again, but unbelievably, all of a sudden, he wasn't bucking, but running. Running flat out, smooth as the wind and twice as fast. He cleared the far fence with daylight showing underneath him.

That was the last thing I saw for a minute, Steve and Rebel sailing over the fence like a centaur. Then, out of nowhere, Russ Donovan's big fist exploded against my teeth and all I could see were red stars. I dropped like a rock.

I shook my head, trying to get my eyes to focus. They did — on Romero. He was on his feet and the gun was back in his hand. He was raising it — and aiming it at the fast-moving horse and rider.

"No!" I screamed. I tried to get up but it was like one of those dreams where the faster you try to run the slower you move. The crack of the pistol shattered the air. I thought I saw Steve jerk in the saddle but he stayed on and Rebel didn't slow down. Another shot rang out, but Steve and Rebel were out of sight, over the hill, and all I could hear was hoofbeats.

Then I heard something else. A voice, right behind me. "All right, Raccoon-Eyes, you just put down that little crackerjack pistol of yours real slow or you're gonna get closely acquainted with a *real* gun."

Pop! I turned to see him standing there, cool as a frog

in November, holding the old 20-gauge shotgun that had hung in our basement as long as we'd been in Fenton. It was so dusty I could see Pop's fingerprints on the stock. I figured if he actually fired it, it would probably blow up. But I guess that looking down its barrel gave a person a whole different perspective. A look of absolute fury crossed Romero's face but I noticed that he turned a little pale. Slowly, he opened his hand and the gun hit the ground with a soft thud.

"Go get it, Raine," Pop said.

Instantly, she ran and picked it up. Russ Donovan started to take a step forward, but Raine swivelled the gun in his direction. "Don't," was all she said, but it was enough to turn him into a statue. She'd use the gun if she had to — and I didn't blame her. These were the guys that had tried to kill my brother. Tried? I thought with a cold twinge deep in my gut. I remembered him lurching in the saddle as the gun fired. What if he was hit?

Pop cocked one eye in my direction. "You okay, Beau?"

"Yeah," I muttered, scrambling to my feet and rubbing my hand across my mouth. I was surprised to find it came away bloody. I wished I had time to hit old Donovan back, but Pop was running the show right now.

"Get over there," he ordered. "Wrap your hands around those corral bars and hang on tight enough to save your life. It just might." Reluctantly, Remoro and Donovan did what they were told. I couldn't help thinking that with their faces cuddled up to the splintery planks like two little kids watching a rodeo through the fence, the two of them looked a lot more silly than dangerous.

"How'd you know they'd be here, Pop?" I asked, trying to fit the pieces of this crazy day together.

"I got home a couple of hours ago and while I was at the house, Hollywood there, with the glasses —" he glared in Romero's direction "— drove in lookin' for Steve. It wasn't too hard to figure out this must be the guy Steve told me about the first night he was home."

"How much did Steve tell you?"

"Not much. Just that he was in some trouble and needed to lie low for a while someplace where this guy wouldn't think of lookin'.

Pop dug his truck keys out of his pocket. "Here," he said, tossing them to me with one hand and keeping the shotgun level with the other. "You better go track your brother down. Give me that pistol, Raine, before you shoot somebody, and go with him. I can handle these two for a while. There's gonna be more cops here than ants at a picnic pretty soon now, anyway."

Twenty-three

*F*ive minutes later Raine and I were bouncing across the pasture field in Pop's Chev. But I wasn't sure where we were going. Steve and Rebel had disappeared. Where was I supposed to start looking? Four or five trails headed off into the woods in different directions. Some were too narrow to get a truck down. Maybe we should have stopped and grabbed a couple of horses.

"How am I supposed to know where he went?" I muttered, breaking the strained silence between Raine and me for the first time.

"I think I know," Raine said softly.

I shot her a glance.

"We, uh, Steve and me, went riding out here a couple of times when you had to stay after school. The first time Steve saw that hillside above the big beaver dam on the north trail he said that's where he'd build a cabin and spend the rest of his life if he had the chance. He said he felt like he belonged there.

"That's where he'd go if he wanted me —" Raine

hesitated and turned kind of red "— if he wanted _us_ to find him."

I didn't say anything. I just turned the truck down the trail to the beaver dam. I knew the place she meant. It was a real nice place. Raine and I go, I mean, we _used_ to go, riding there all the time . . .

The trail narrowed and I stopped the truck. We walked the rest of the way in silence. A million thoughts were churning through my mind. What was going to happen to Steve now? What did I _want_ to happen to him? And Raine and Steve. Was what Steve had tried to tell me true? Was the ghost of Tracey all he was seeing in Raine? But what was Raine seeing in him?

My mind was so far away as I walked along, head down, that I didn't even notice that we'd turned the corner to where the valley opened out until Raine brought me back to reality.

"Look!" she said suddenly, and started to run.

I looked. It was just like a calendar picture spread out below, with the still, dark water of the dam reflecting the sky and the last gold of the falling leaves. And standing there on the bank, holding the shining black horse, his own hair gold in the late-fall sunshine, stood my brother. I started to run too.

Rebel's ears shot up as he heard us coming and Steve slowly turned to face us. "Steve! You're all right!" Raine said, throwing her arms around him.

Wincing, Steve returned the hug — with his left arm.

"Ouch," he said softly, giving Raine a teasing grin. "You're just as dangerous when you like me as when you hate me."

"What?" Raine said, stepping back so I could see that the right sleeve of Steve's jean jacket was dark with blood.

"So Romero didn't miss," I said.

Steve glanced at his arm and shrugged. "Didn't do much damage. It stings a little and it's bleeding some but he didn't hit anything real vital. What happened to Romero and Donovan?"

"Pop happened," I said. "He showed up with that old cannon he keeps hanging in the basement and tidied things up like he was the sheriff of Dodge City. Last I saw, the two of them were holding hands with a corral rail and waiting for the cops to show."

Steve laughed. "I figured that's about what would happen. I saw Pop coming before I hit the saddle."

"Which," I interrupted, "was about your stupidest move yet. What if Rebel had unloaded you right in Romero's lap?"

"Stupid is the way I operate. Hadn't you noticed? Anyhow, I knew Rebel was losin' interest in bucking, weren't you, Reb?" He gave the horse a friendly slap on the shoulder. Then he held out the reins to Raine. "I think it's safe to take him home now. I've got a feeling the horse sale kind of disintegrated about the time the shooting started. If you and Beau keep workin' with him he should be downright domesticated before J.C. can get any more big ideas about selling him."

"What are you gonna do now?" Raine asked, her voice going kind of hoarse.

Steve was silent for a minute. "I don't know," he said slowly. Then, "How'd you guys get out here?"

"Pop's truck's at the end of the trail."

"Let's go get it." The four of us walked down the trail with only the sound of the leaves rustling under our feet. Even Rebel, who'd had a good long run, was quiet for once.

We reached the truck.

"Got the keys, Beau?"

"Yeah."

Steve held out his hand for them but I hesitated. "If I get going now," he said, "I can make it out the back way to the next road before the cops discover there's a warrant out on me for breaking parole."

"Or," I said slowly, "you could just come home with us and turn yourself in."

For a minute Steve and I just looked at each other. But then he shook his head. "Can't do it, Beau. Not here. Not now. I need some more time."

"Time for what?" I said angrily. "Running some more?"

"You gonna try and stop me, Beau?"

"Did anything I ever did stop you before?"

"Not exactly," he said with a grin. "But that tackle you used on Romero could sure slow a guy down." Then his face turned serious. "Thanks for everything, Beau. I'll be back sometime when I get my head straight."

"Sure, Steve," I said, totally unconvinced.

Steve held out his hand — the left one of course. "Trust me, Beau," he said, his voice teasing.

I broke down and returned his grin. "Yeah, Steve, I trust you — like a piranha." But we shook hands on it.

Then Steve turned to Raine. "So just like that you drive away into nowhere," she said, fighting hard to control her voice. "You'll probably bleed to death out there somewhere."

Steve looked at his arm, which was still oozing a little blood. "No, I won't," he said. "Not if you could sacrifice that designer scarf for a bandage, rich girl."

Even through the tears, the flash of Raine's eyes was unmistakable. "Don't you dare call me that!" she said, but she took off her scarf — which I'd seen her buy at K-Mart for $2.99. Steve held out his arm and she wrapped the scarf around a couple of times and tied it.

Steve laughed at her. "Where'd you suddenly learn

to be gentle? It's supposed to stop the bleeding, not make me look like a rock singer. Tie it tight."

Raine shot him a dangerous look, untied the knot, and jerked it as tight as she could. Steve winced, then nodded. "That's better," he said.

He and Raine stood looking at each other. I heard Raine take a deep breath. She wiped her sleeve across her eyes and when she spoke again her voice held a hint of the old challenge. "The scarf's a loan, not a gift."

"You got it, lady." Steve bent down to kiss her on the cheek. It was the kind of kiss you'd give your sister — or maybe even your brother's girl.

Steve got in the truck. He reached in his pocket and brought out something that he handed out the window to me. It was thirty dollars. "Give this to Pop for me. And tell him thanks. I'll park the truck in Calgary and send him home the keys."

He started to drive away and then stopped again. "You better not put any scratches on my purple car while I'm gone." He gunned the engine and the Chev rattled away, leaving Raine and me alone in the settling dust.

The two of us stood watching the truck as it turned into a tiny brown bug with a plume of dust behind it. Then it was over a hill and there was nothing left to see. Steve was gone and it was just Raine and me again. But I wasn't so sure that we could ever be the same two people we were before he came.

"So," I said, finally breaking the heavy silence, "where does that leave us?"

Raine looked up at me, trying hard not to cry. "What do you mean, Beau?"

"You're still in love with him, aren't you?"

A lot of things had changed in the last two months. But one thing hadn't. Raine's honesty. The look she gave me was level and straight. "Yeah, Beau, I guess I'll always be kind of in love with your brother."

I swallowed. "So I guess we're not going together any more, huh?" I was surprised at how much this could still hurt after everything we'd been through.

"I guess that's up to you."

I stared at her. "What's that supposed to mean?"

"Steve just rode into the sunset," she said slowly. "Some day I'm going to wake up and ask myself if he was real at all."

I waited for her to go on. "You're real, Beau. Always there when I need you." She paused uncertainly and her gaze dropped to the patch of ground she was scuffing with a dusty boot. Then she looked up and her eyes met mine. "You're the best friend I ever had. Is that good enough for now, Beau?"

Was it? I looked into those deep, stormy-sea grey eyes of hers and tried to make up my mind. I put my arm around her shoulders and we started down the trail for home.

Printed in Canada